CHALLENGES FOR JILL

'Excellent job for two young girls
knowledgeable with horses. Live in ...'

This advertisement in the local
newspaper seems the chance of a
lifetime to Jill Crewe and Ann Derry.
The reality, however, turns out to be
nine wild New Forest ponies, which they
are expected to break in. Fortunately
their motto is 'Never say die', but they
have several adventures before their
return home.

Challenges for Jill

Ruby Ferguson

KNIGHT BOOKS
Hodder and Stoughton

Text copyright © 1960 by Hodder and Stoughton Ltd

First published in 1960 by Hodder
and Stoughton Ltd

This edition first published as
Pony Jobs for Jill in 1973
by Knight Books

Eleventh impression 1984

Set, printed and bound in Great Britain for
Hodder and Stoughton Paperbacks, a
division of Hodder and Stoughton Ltd.,
Mill Road, Dunton Green, Sevenoaks,
Kent (Editorial Office: 47 Bedford
Square, London, WC1 3DP) by
Cox & Wyman Ltd, Reading

ISBN 0 340 36708 3

Contents

1　Just the job!　　　　　　　　　　　7

2　Welcome to Little Chimneys　　　14

3　The comic set-up　　　　　　　　25

4　An awful lot of pony　　　　　　38

5　The new idea　　　　　　　　　　49

6　It's Cecilia　　　　　　　　　　　59

7　Wasn't it murder?　　　　　　　73

8　Brushing up the team　　　　　　85

9　The Usefull Charmes　　　　　　96

10　Lucky again　　　　　　　　　111

11　Two duds　　　　　　　　　　120

12　Mysterious　　　　　　　　　131

13　Shock after shock　　　　　　142

14　The point-to-point　　　　　　152

I
Just the job!

'CAST your gorgeous orbs on that,' exclaimed my friend Ann Derry, slapping a folded newspaper down in front of me and pointing to a small ad which she had outlined in red pencil. 'Isn't it the tops? Just what we want.'

With my long and disillusioning experience I did not at once burst into cheers. I had come to take a poor view of what other people thought was the tops.

I don't know if you have noticed, but other people's idea of bliss is seldom yours. I once went to stay with my cousin Cecilia (a square if ever there was one) and after whipping up my excitement about a smashing day out, I discovered that her idea of heaven was walking round an art gallery looking at some pictures of women made out of cubes with two eyes on the same side, followed by China tea and toast at a gruesome café called Ye Olde Cathedral Tea Shoppe.

I am not one to bear every wrong with patience, as the hymn says, so I complained loudly, and Cecilia said, 'Well, what *do* you like?'

I said, 'What about packing up a picnic hamper and inducing your mother to run us in the car to the nearest beach, and then do a spot of rock climbing?' and she said, 'That suits me.'

Once again I was to be disillusioned.

Cecilia's idea of a picnic was a glossy hamper full of gleaming cups and plates and knives and spoons, and glass dishes to fill with dainty sandwiches, etc.

It took us over an hour to make the dainty sandwiches and pack the dainty cakes for this outfit, and all the time we were eating Cecilia kept on fussing and counting the knives in case one got lost in the sand, and by then I had lost interest in rock climbing, and we packed the wretched hamper up and lugged it home and spent half the evening washing it up ready for the next time. I took jolly good care that so far as I was concerned there wasn't going to be any next time. So it just shows.

So when Ann came bouncing in full of girlish enthusiasm to make the remark with which this story begins, I merely said coldly, 'Well, what is it, anyway?'

'It's a job,' she said. 'Smasher. Just what you and I are looking for to fill in the next six months.'

I must at this stage explain that Ann and I were at this time in the awful state of being neither one thing nor the other. We had passed (or scraped through) our GCE and left school, and we weren't ready to go and train for any serious job or profession. Actually we weren't quite sure what we wanted to do. When we told our parents this they went on like mad about 'any girl who isn't an absolute clot knows what she wants to do at sixteen', but to our surprise our headmistress backed us up and said that it was because we were so versatile and lively-minded that we couldn't decide between all the fascinating careers in which we were bound eventually to shine.

However, there was still about six months to fill in. If left to ourselves we could have filled it in very nicely, helping in various stables and riding other people's show jumpers, but that idea was coldly received. No, we had got to do something useful for later life, and what could be more useful to a girl than domestic science? There happened to be a domestic science school in Ryechester and we could go every day.

'Think,' said Mummy, 'of the future. A girl can't learn too young how to run a home.'

Ann and I weren't excited because, between you and me, we'd much rather have had the prospect of running a stable than a home.

Ann said, 'What do we do at this place, for instance?'

'Paper ceilings,' I said. 'Very tricky.'

'And cooking, I suppose?'

'Oh gosh yes,' I said. 'They chain you to a cooker till your eyebrows fall off into the soup.'

'Well, it isn't my cup of tea,' said Ann, 'and I can't think it's yours, Jill. Tell you what, let's get ourselves a job where we're at least self-supporting, and then nobody can grumble.'

'Find one,' I said cynically. 'Just you find one!'

And now it seems she'd found one.

I read the ad. It said, 'Excellent job for two young girls knowledgeable with horses. Live in. Apply Little Chimneys Farm, Blowmore, Hants.'

'There you are,' said Ann. 'Made to measure. Live in. We'd be self-supporting and have the time of our lives messing about with other people's horses, and it wouldn't cost us a dime.'

'What about my own ponies?' I said.

'Take them with us. I'd ride one and you the other. You'd get them supported too, and no food bills.'

I said I'd think about it.

'I don't know what's the matter with you, Jill Crewe,' Ann said. 'But I'll tell you one thing. There'll be about a million girls knowledgeable about horses after this job, and unless we clinch it here and now we'll have lost the chance of a lifetime.'

'Oh, don't talk like my cousin Cecilia,' I said. 'Okay, we'd better go and tell the parents.'

Our mothers said what might be expected. That

if it was really a good job they wouldn't stand in our way of being self-reliant, etc., etc., but they'd have to know an awful lot about our employer in case he turned out to be another Squeers.

I rushed up to Mrs Darcy's, and said, 'Look, you know practically everybody horsy within a hundred miles. Do you know anything about this Little Chimneys Farm?'

As it happened she did. It was kept by somebody called Captain Sound, and he was perfectly respectable.

Having heard this our mothers told us we could apply, so we sat down to write the letter. We did it about ten times, and finally composed this.

Dear Sir,

We were very interested in your advertisement and would like to apply for your job. We are two girls very experienced with the horse in sickness, health, and everything else. We have both had a lifetime of show riding and looking after our own ponies, and we have also taught riding and practically run a riding school single-handed. We are both very intelligent and fond of hard work as long as it is with horses. What we are looking for is a living-in job where we can be self-supporting until we can decide what sort of careers to take up. The following people will give us first-class references –

We then wrote down the names of everybody we could think of, such as Mrs Darcy, Captain Cholly-Sawcutt, and the local M.F.H.

'It sounds terrific,' I said. 'That ought to jolly well fetch them. I bet all those other millions of girls won't have anything like our qualifications.'

We posted the letter and waited breathlessly. A few days later Captain Sound replied. He asked us if we would like to come over for an interview, but suggested that as we were both so jolly good an interview might not be necessary as he was satisfied we'd do, so if we were prepared to come and start work that would be okay by him.

Ann and I were for starting then and there, but at this stage Ann's mother put a spoke in the wheel by asking how much wages we were going to get. Ann said that not having sordid minds, and caring for nothing but the noble cause of equitation, we had not thought of such a thing, and Ann's mother said, rubbish, and that was just like us, absolutely no more idea than babies, and Ann must ring up Captain Sound immediately and find out.

So very reluctantly Ann did, hoping Captain Sound would not think we had miserly natures, but he took it quite calmly and said he had thought of four pounds.

Ann said that suited us, and in spite of her mother grumbling and saying that it was ridiculous to let him think that we had no business instincts, we got our way, packed Black Boy and Rapide into a horse-box, threw a few horsy garments into our suitcases, and set out for Little Chimneys Farm.

2

Welcome to Little Chimneys

'WHAT do you think the farm is going to look like?' asked Ann.

As usual sticking my neck out, I said, 'Oh, I should think frightfully Children-of-the-New-Forest-ish, an ancient stone house with mullion windows and window seats and pewter plates all over the shop, and one of those wells that make an awful row when you pull the bucket up.'

'As long as *we* don't have to pull the bucket up –!' said Ann.

Well, of course, I was dead wrong. There wasn't anything farmy-looking at all about Little Chimneys Farm, in fact it was a large tinny bungalow, with bits of extra rooms like huts stuck on all over the place, and it was wedged in between two fir copses on the main road. We couldn't mistake it because there was a large board nailed to a tree at the road-end of a cinder track, with the name on.

'Crumbs!' said Ann.

At that moment Mrs Sound came running down the cinder path to greet us. She couldn't have been more welcoming if we had been her long-lost nieces, and we certainly felt we were wanted. She was obviously slightly wacky and was wearing blue slacks, a pink jumper, and four rows of pearl beads.

'Which is Ann and which is Jill?' she asked. We told her, but from then on she never got it right, in fact half the time she was calling us Amy and Judy.

'Well, come in,' she said. 'We didn't expect you quite so soon and my husband hasn't got home yet, so you don't have to start on the ponies right away, do you?'

Actually we didn't feel like starting on the ponies right away, as we were hungry and had hopes of a cup of cocoa or something similarly cheering, so without further discussion we followed Mrs Sound into the house.

It was the most comic house, a living-room with bits of rooms, sheds, huts, cupboards, and what-have-yous, stuck on at unexpected angles. For instance, to get to our bedroom Ann and I had to go through a store-hut full of bags of chicken food.

'This is yours,' said Mrs Sound. 'Such a dear little room.'

I felt like saying, 'Where's the floor?' because you couldn't see any, it was so taken up with furniture. There was a large double bed, a colossal wardrobe that I'm sure fifteen people could have kept their clothes in, a chest of drawers with two of the drawers permanently stuck out because they wouldn't go in, two chairs, and a bookcase, the sort that has glass doors and shelves going up and up to the ceiling with no books on them.

Ann and I just stood there stunned, and Mrs Sound must have thought we were dumb with admiration because she said, 'So glad you like it.'

'Is the bathroom anywhere near?' I asked when I found my voice.

Mrs Sound said, oh yes, it was just back through the chicken-food store and across the living-room, and through the door next to the window, and up three steps, and the second door you came to, very handy.

Ann began to giggle, and turned it into a frightful fit of coughing.

Mrs Sound said, was there anything she could get her, and I felt like saying, 'Yes, a cup of cocoa,' but daren't, and Mrs Sound said, 'Well, it's only a quarter to twelve and we don't have lunch till one, so that gives you time to get unpacked. You'll find lots of room for your things. I *do* like to have lots of room for my things.'

There was certainly lots of room for our things, in fact when our joint collection of garments was stowed away in the enormous wardrobe and drawers it was barely noticeable; but what we needed was room for people. One of us had to sit on the bed all the time, while the other one did a steeplechase over the rest of the furniture. We were now more or less hysterical with laughing as well as hungry, so we wandered back to the living-room where there was nobody to be seen; however, there was a lot of clattering going on in the distance, which proved to be two huts away where Mrs Sound was gaily cooking lunch and reading *Pride and Prejudice* at the same time, which was propped up against the gas cooker.

She looked exactly like the duchess in *Alice in Wonderland* making the soup, especially as she kept on grabbing two little tins without looking at them and shaking them over whatever she was cooking.

At last she looked round and said, 'I say, would you two girls mind frightfully laying the table? I've got to go on stirring this ragout, and I've just got to the bit where Mr Collins proposes to Elizabeth so I can't leave it.'

We said we'd lay the table with pleasure if she'd tell us where the things were, and she said vaguely, 'Well, I never quite know myself, but everything's in the drawers in the living-room, if you just keep looking until you find it.'

So after going through practically every drawer in the place we eventually got the table laid, though we couldn't imagine why Mrs Sound didn't make some attempt at least to keep the knives, forks, and spoons in the same drawer; and went back to the kitchen to find our hostess fishing *Pride and Prejudice* out of the ragout into which it had just fallen.

At last a car drove up. It was Captain Sound. He was a very smart-looking man and immaculately dressed, and he shook hands with us as if we were about twenty-one and said, 'Welcome to Little Chimneys.'

We said, 'Hallo.'

'If I may say so,' said Captain Sound, 'you look very workmanlike. I like to see girls who work in a riding-stable *dressed* like girls who work in a riding-stable and not like art students.'

Ann and I didn't know what to say, as we always did wear jodhs and shirts and pullovers, and weren't sure what art students wore anyway, so we didn't say anything but merely smiled intelligently.

One thing I was glad to know was that we were going to work in a riding-stable, because up to then we hadn't been quite sure.

'Do you want to come out and see the ponies now?' said Captain Sound, 'or do you want to have lunch first?'

Ann and I looked at one another. All the time we seemed to be getting side-tracked away from food, and by now we felt like famished explorers, so Ann muttered something about lunch being ready and perhaps Mrs Sound wouldn't want it to be kept waiting, which I thought was pretty cunning of her.

'Good, good!' said Captain Sound. 'Then let us to the feast. Sit down, sit down.'

He sat down at the top of the table and waved us to either side, and in came Mrs Sound with the ragout.

There was plenty of it, but, as we feared, it tasted slightly of *Pride and Prejudice* and very much of salt and pepper.

'Potatoes?' said Captain Sound. 'Who's hiding the potatoes?'

'Oh dear,' said Mrs Sound, 'I forgot to do any.'

'Never mind,' said our employer, 'perhaps you remembered to do a nice pudding?'

Mrs Sound looked quite pathetically at Ann and me, and said, 'Now how can I have possibly forgotten to do a pudding, but I'm afraid I did. But there's some cake in the tin.'

'No there isn't,' said the Captain. 'We ate it last night, don't you remember? When you forgot to order a tin of spaghetti for supper.'

'Of course!' said Mrs Sound, brightening up. 'Well, we'll just have to have a nice cup of coffee. There isn't any milk, but who wants milk!'

Ann and I daren't look at each other for fear of exploding.

At this moment there was an interruption, as the horse van arrived with my two ponies.

'What's this? What's this?' said Captain Sound.

'Actually, it's my own two ponies,' I explained. 'I thought it would be all right to have them here, as they'll provide transport for Ann and me, and I don't mind them being used in the riding-school under my supervision.'

'Oh, that's all right,' said Captain Sound. 'They can go in with the others. You'll find them very useful when you have to do a bit of rodeo work.'

'Rodeo work!' I said, with my eyes popping out.

'Oh, you know. Rounding up the other ponies, and so on.'

In all my lifetime of experience I had never worked in a riding-school where you had to use two ponies to round up the others. This sounded more like a circus than a riding-school; however, one has to get used to other methods so I didn't comment.

'Excuse us, please,' I said, and Ann and I went out and helped the man to lead Black Boy and Rapide out of the van and down the ramp.

They both looked a bit peeved and surprised, as they had only ridden in a horse van two or three times in their lives, and then it was to emerge in a nice, grassy park at a show. Now they were standing in the road outside Little Chimneys Farm and staring round as if they wondered where on earth they had got to.

Captain Sound came out and joined us.

'If I may say so, a very nice pair of ponies,' he remarked. 'Which one belongs to which?'

'Actually they're both mine,' I said. 'I've had them ever since I was a kid. Ann's mother has just sold her pony because he was too small for Ann.'

(I may add that Ann's mother is the kind of person who sells ponies as soon as she considers they are grown out of, just as if they were old shoes, and I cannot approve of this. Neither can Ann, but she doesn't get any say.)

'I should think they're very well schooled,' said Captain Sound.

'I should jolly well hope so!' I said. 'I've been working on them for years and they've both won heaps of prizes.'

'They weren't up to much when Jill got them,' said Ann, 'so she gets the credit for making them so good.'

'Splendid, splendid!' said Captain Sound. 'I can see these two ponies are going to be a great asset to us, as well as Jill's schooling ability. Let's fasten them here to the railings for the time being and go and have a look at the rest of the gang.'

Feeling rather full of ragout and of nothing else, Ann and I followed him. If we were expecting to see a row of neat stables we were disappointed, as there seemed to be nothing behind the house but hens and hen-houses. He led us round these, and at the back was a large field, and we gave a gasp.

The field was full of ponies. Wild ponies. New Forest ponies. There were nine of them, trotting about gaily and all turning their heads in our direction.

'Golly!' said Ann. 'They're *wild* ponies.'

We must both have looked a bit stunned, because Captain Sound said hastily, 'Not so wild. Just nice, raw material. You can make anything of these.'

'B-B-B-But –' I stammered.

'Oh, I've put in a lot of work on them,' he said. 'They're all used to the halter. Nice friendly little things, they are.'

'I bet they are,' I said, 'but what about being broken to the saddle?'

'Oh come,' he said, 'that'll be nothing to experts like we three. We must get to work. I can see us having high jinks with this crowd.'

'Too right. So can I,' muttered Ann to me, as Captain Sound produced a bag of apples from his pocket and began breaking them up for the ponies who came crowding round the gate, looking slyly at us with their pretty, mischievous faces.

'Have you had them on a lungeing rope?' I asked doubtfully.

'Why, of course. At least, most of them. They're

really at the stage of getting saddles on their backs and we'll soon manage that.'

It struck me that Captain Sound was something of an optimist, and I understood his reference to a rodeo, only I didn't fancy the idea of my own ponies being used to round up nine dear little flying hooves.

'I should think it's going to be a long time before they'll be any good for riding-school work,' said Ann.

'Oh, not a bit. They're very intelligent.'

'They've got to be more than intelligent, they've got to be jolly reliable and steady,' I pointed out, 'before you can put small kids on them.'

'Ah now, my dear young lady, we mustn't make difficulties,' said Captain Sound. 'As I said before, we're all experts, aren't we? And I'm quite sure that two fine horsewomen like yourself and Ann aren't going to be beaten by a bunch of fresh little ponies.'

Put like that he had us in what might be called a cleft stick. We couldn't let ourselves down by admitting failure.

'We'll do what we can, of course,' I said.

'Splendid, splendid. Now I suggest that this afternoon we put a lungeing rope on each of them in turn, and pick out the most adaptable, and those can try a bit of road work. You two can each ride one of Jill's ponies and lead a couple of these.'

'I hope the roads are quiet,' said Ann.

'Oh, perfectly quiet, just lots of nice lanes.'

'Meanwhile,' I said, 'where do I park my ponies? I can't leave them tied to the railings for long or they'll get restive.'

'I suppose they're used to being out at grass?' said Captain Sound.

'During the summer, yes,' I said, as it was quite obvious to me then that there weren't any stables at Little Chimneys Farm, and winter was coming on.

'Well, pop them in here with the others. They'll get used to each other that way and the trained ponies will do the untrained ones good.'

I could feel my eyes opening as big as saucers at this peculiar idea, and for the first time I began to wonder just how much Captain Sound really knew about ponies.

'That's impossible,' I said, trying not to sound rude. 'The wild pones will kick mine. They might even gang up and attack them.'

'In that case,' said Captain Sound, 'there's another little field at the side of the house. Yours can go in there.'

'Thanks very much,' I said. 'I think I'll go and get them settled. They'll be a bit nappy after the journey and needing some peace and quiet. Come on, Ann.'

3
The comic set-up

'WELL, what do you make of this set-up?' I said to Ann as we walked round the house.

'It's comic,' she said. 'I think Captain and Mrs Sound are both slightly mad, but they seem kind and it may be fun. Actually I've always wanted to break in a New Forest pony.'

'Oh, me too,' I said. 'But I hope he doesn't think we can get them to riding-school standard in about three weeks. It'll take ages before you can put a small child on any of them.'

'Between you and me,' said Ann, 'I don't think he knows an awful lot about horses.'

'That's what I'm thinking,' I said. 'Therefore he's relying on us for everything. Crumbs! When he talked about a riding-school I had visions of – well, a riding-school! But this is jolly well starting from scratch. Raw material! Gosh!'

'And there aren't any stables,' said Ann, 'which means he intends to keep them permanently out at grass, which won't help with their training, and they'll never be clipped all the winter. It'll be a funny riding-school with unclipped ponies.'

'Don't worry,' I said. 'It'll be next summer after a hard winter's work before this outfit can invite customers.'

'Coo!' said Ann. 'I wonder if we'll last that long?'

'Oh, never say die,' I said. 'Only I do hope Mrs Sound doesn't forget the spaghetti again tonight. I'm still hungry.'

We collected my ponies and turned them into the small field, which wasn't bad and had shady trees along one side, though the whole field was on a slope and Ann said she hoped that Black Boy and Rapide wouldn't develop one leg shorter than the other through walking sideways.

'Sorry, boys!' I said cheerfully as I patted their cheeks and let them nuzzle my hand. 'You'll have to make do with this. At least the grass looks lush.'

We went back to find Captain Sound, and there he was lungeing a small grey pony.

'This one's coming on nicely,' he said lightheartedly. 'And I think those other three are ready for some road work. How about it, girls? Would you care to trot them out and see how they behave?'

I stared at him.

'But they're not shod!' I said.

He looked taken back. Then he looked down at the ponies' feet as if he expected them suddenly to grow shoes, or wondered why they had not been born with them on.

'Oh, of course,' he said. 'I ought to have taken them to the farrier this morning. I wonder if you'd lead them along there now. It's only about half a mile.'

We said we'd better do it at once, so we took the three ponies by their halters and set off.

'Well, this is comic,' said Ann. 'I'm beginning to wonder if he even knew that ponies had to be shod. He seems very loose in the brain, when it comes to horses.'

'And Mrs Sound seems very loose in the brain when it comes to housekeeping,' I added. 'If there's a shop near the farrier's we'd better buy some chocolate in case she does forget the supper.'

They were charming ponies, small-boned and pretty, with the most lovely mischievous eyes, and they didn't behave badly at all on the way except for a bit of titupping. They probably recognized that they were in the hands of experience.

When we got to the farrier's he took one look and said, 'Blimey, what's this little lot?'

I didn't care for his attitude and replied coldly, 'I want to have these ponies shod, please. And send the account to Captain Sound.'

'Huh!' he said. 'I'll send the account to Mister Captain Sound if you like, and if it isn't settled in a week I'll be coming round to know why. I heard he'd bought a herd of New Forest ponies for about twenty quid, but I didn't believe it till now. Thinks he's going to start a riding-school and make a fortune. How mad can a chap get?'

'I see you're not busy,' I said. 'We'll wait.'

'Oh, you will, will you? And who may you be?'

'We're professionals,' said Ann. 'We train ponies and run riding-schools and teach riding. We've been doing it for years, and we know what we're talking about, and we're not to be trifled with.'

The farrier said Ha-ha in a hollow sort of voice and added, 'Blimey, what sort of an animal do you call that one? The Thing from Outer Space?'

The one he was pointing at was certainly a very peculiar colour, a kind of mauve-y roan if you can imagine it, and very long in the back, but I suddely felt a great affection for this animal welling up in my noble breast, and replied heatedly, 'Actually that's my favourite, and it's called Happy Dawn.'

'Blow me down!' said the farrier. 'Well, come along, let's get cracking.'

I must admit he had quite a picnic shoeing those ponies, as you can imagine. They did everything but tie themselves in knots and Ann and I hung on until we were breathless. He must have been a pretty good farrier because eventually they were done and we were picking bits of the floor out of our hair.

I said to Ann, 'I'll see that the rest are much more under control before we bring them along here.

Captain Sound knows nothing, and I'll not take his word for anything in future.'

The ponies didn't like their new shoes and behaved like temperamental Russian ballerinas all the way home. We were so occupied that we didn't have time to think about buying chocolate.

When we got back Captain Sound said, 'Oh, you have been a long time.'

Ann said, 'If you know how long it takes to shoe a docile horse you can just multiply it by ten for these. I'm afraid they're not as ready for the road as you think, and they hate their shoes. Is there anywhere we can put them until they get used to being shod? They might start lashing out, and injure the others.'

'We could tether them in the yard for the night,' he said.

'I don't think that's an awfully good idea,' I said. 'It might make them very upset. If you have any kind of stable or outhouse I could put my own ponies in, and these could go in the little field.'

'Well, there's a very big pigsty,' he said, 'if your ponies wouldn't mind.'

He took us and showed us, and it really was an enormous pigsty. It made me wonder how many and what sort of pigs had originally been kept there, but I said, 'This will do nicely for my ponies, if you can give us some water and brooms to clean it out, and some straw.'

Apparently there were some brooms Somewhere and some straw Somewhere. It took us about half an hour to find out where Somewhere was. We then got to work, and although the bucket leaked we finally had the place cleaned up.

'I must say, you are workers,' said Captain Sound. 'Now come along in and have your supper.'

No words could have been sweeter music to our ears, especially as nobody had suggested tea, and it was now about seven o'clock. We fetched my ponies in and settled them down, and turned the three newly-shod ones into the small field. Then we went into the house, and washed and put on clean cotton dresses.

Eagerly we filtered into the living-room, but there was no sign of supper, the table wasn't even laid.

Captain Sound said, 'It won't be a minute.'

'Okay,' we said.

Then Mrs Sound appeared from the kitchen with *Pride and Prejudice* in her hand.

'Oh dear,' she said. 'It's never supper time?'

'Can we help?' said Ann.

'Well, I don't see how you can,' said Mrs Sound, 'because actually there doesn't seem to be anything – I mean, we could have eggs, couldn't we? If Amy and Judy like eggs.'

'Ann and I could make omelettes,' I suggested. Anything to get the food situation moving.

'Oh, how kind of you,' said Mrs Sound. 'I do hope the Calor gas hasn't run out as I forgot to tell them to send another cylinder.'

We hoped so too! Fortunately it lasted while I made the omelettes and Ann knocked up a sponge pudding, but while the pudding was cooking the gas conked out. Fortunately there was plenty of bread, and we found a half pound of butter that Mrs Sound didn't know was there. We then gobbled up this meagre repast, and I muttered to Ann, 'Us for the village shop tomorrow, and lay in a private hoard and a tin-opener.'

Next morning we asked if there was a saddler's in the village and there was, so we suggested we might buy some cleaning tack and Captain Sound agreed it was a good idea and gave us two pound notes.

The shop wasn't really a saddler's but a corn chandler's selling cattle food, poultry food, and farming odds and ends, but they kept brushes, saddle soap, and stable rubbers, so we bought what we needed, and then made a bee-line for the grocer's. There we laid in tins of biscuits, chocolate bars, and fruit which could be eaten in bed on Mrs Sound's more forgetful days, and made a big hole in our spending money.

As we ambled back, Ann on Black Boy and me on Rapide, Ann said, 'I say, we ought to write to our fond mammas today to say we've arrived. What shall we say?'

'Well, we'd better not tell them about Mrs Sound forgetting to feed us, or Captain Sound being scatty,' I said, 'or they'll tell us to come home jolly quick. We shall have to concoct a letter with the utmost cunning.'

Ann said that when it came to diplomacy, cunning, and tactful documents she was streets ahead of me, so she would write the letter, and I could copy it.

In the afternoon Captain Sound insisted that we should take the three shod ponies out for a bit of roadwork, but I finally persuaded him to make it only two, the mauve-y roan one which I had recklessly named Happy Dawn, and a cute little foxy-coloured one on whom needless to say we quickly bestowed the name Merry Night.

'All right,' he said, 'I'll go round to the small field and catch them while you two get ready.'

Five minutes later Ann and I arrived at the small field to behold a sensational sight, Captain Sound leaping wildly about the field while the ponies gaily danced and kicked up their heels just out of his reach.

'I can't catch them,' he said crossly. 'I've never had this trouble before. It must have made them a bit wild when they went to be shod.'

I knew he was only saying this to save his face, because he must have had loads of trouble before.

Ann said, 'If you'll excuse me saying so, you

should never try to catch a pony by chasing it. You'll only scare and excite it, and then you'll never catch it. And honestly, you shouldn't wave the halter.'

'Well, what would you advise?' said Captain Sound. 'These are exceptional ponies.'

'It really applies to any pony with spirit,' I said. 'Push the halter down your coat and hold out an apple or a carrot and be very quiet until you've induced the pony to come to you. Then while he's eating the apple you can gently slip the halter on, and quietly lead him away. He won't mind coming a bit, because there's been nothing to startle him.'

'I ought to have tethered them,' he said.

'Oh gosh no!' said Ann. 'They get all tied up in the ropes and go frantic. Shall Jill and I have a go at catching the two we want?'

Captain Sound was only too glad to let us have a go, but by now the ponies were thoroughly upset and knew what we were after, so we had no end of a job to make them interested in apples.

It almost felt like a rest cure when we were finally out on the road, Ann riding Black Boy and leading Merry Night, and I on Rapide and leading Happy Dawn. It was a pleasant, sunny afternoon with no wind, and we kept to the lanes of which there were plenty, letting the ponies use the grass verges as much as they could. The two wild ponies showed temperament all the time and we had to hold them closely, also our arms got very tired from keeping their heads up as their one idea was to stop and crop grass, but they were attractive ponies and we grew quite fond of them. Also, though I say it without boasting, they did recognize the hand of experience and didn't behave badly at all. When an unexpected lorry appeared round a bend Ann said, 'Now for it!' but nothing desperate happened. As you know, New Forest ponies do wander on the local roads and get used to seeing traffic.

'We might even make riding-school ponies out of these,' said Ann cheerfully, 'in about umpteen years.'

When we got back, the pair of them walked in beautifully, Happy Dawn having a pretty natural action and Merry Night picking up his feet well.

'I say, they do look good,' said Captain Sound. 'We'll have those two saddled up in no time.'

(That's what you think! I thought.)

'Now what about a cup of tea, and then taking another pair to be shod?'

We groaned, not at the welcome idea of a cup of tea, but because we were aching already, but we didn't like to look unwilling.

We all went into the house, and there being no sign of Mrs Sound we made the tea ourselves, and then fled into our bedroom and ate a few of our biscuits. We then straightened our backs and prepared to take two more ponies to the farrier.

The two we took gave us a lot of trouble. If there is one thing I do not enjoy in the world of horses it is hanging on to the end of a rope with a dancing pony at the other end, doing his best to pull me up into the air. However, we stopped by a strip of common and let them dance until they were tired, and then proceeded to the village.

'Wot! Not you again?' said the farrier.

'Don't get excited,' said Ann. 'There are four more to come.'

'Coo!' he said. 'Somebody's gone crackers.'

We kept cool, and after a gruesome struggle that lot were finally shod, and we arrived back at Little Chimneys feeling like chewed string.

'I vote we call these two Mustard and Pepper,' I suggested. 'No romantic names for them.'

We turned the two into the small field with the other three shod ones, and took my ponies to the glorified pigsty where we rubbed them down and gave them a feed.

We were surprised to see no one about, and when we got to the house, though everything was open, there was nobody there. Then we saw a note on the table, 'Please feed chickens, gone to the pictures, your supper is in the oven.'

We thought it was a bit casual of the Sounds, just going off and leaving everything.

'I vote we get supper before we feed the chickens,' said Ann. 'I think it's a bit thick, Mrs Sound could at least have done that job before she went out. It isn't our work.'

When we looked in the oven we found a cheese and tomato pie, but Mrs Sound had left the gas too high and it was nearly dried up.

I said darkly, 'I don't believe they've gone to the pictures at all. I think they've gone out to get a decent meal. I can just see them now, sitting in front of roast beef and Yorkshire pudding and –'

'That's enough of that,' said Ann.

We ate the dry pie, and made a pot of tea, as there didn't seem to be any coffee in the house. Then we went and fed all the ponies, and the chickens, and put the chickens in for the night.

'We've still got to write those letters home,' said Ann.

It felt like the last straw. We got a writing pad out and Ann went into a sort of trance for about twenty minutes. Then she said: 'This is the best I can do. My brain feels addled.'

I read it.

It said:

Dear Mummy,

  This is just to let you know that we have arrived safely. The country round here is lovely and just right for riding. We have nine ponies to look after as well as Jill's so we are kept very busy but it is out of doors all the time which is very

*nice. The grocer's shop in the village is called
Webster's which is the same as ours at home, isn't
that funny?*

No more now, tons of love,

Ann.

'H'm,' I said. 'Sounds a bit gruesome to me. I
don't know about your mother, but mine won't be
exactly thrilled to get that. However, I'm too tired
to do anything about it, so I'll just copy it and let's
go to bed.'

By then it was nine o'clock and dark, and we
wondered whether we ought to lock the door of the
house before we went to bed. It really was a bit
thick of the Sounds to leave us like this, not knowing what to do. In the end we didn't lock it, as we
didn't want them banging us up after we'd gone to
sleep.

We couldn't have baths as Mrs Sound hadn't
thought of making up the boiler before she went out
and the water was cold, so we rolled grumbling into
bed. I may add that the bed was a feather one and
you went down and down into a sort of tunnel
among the feathers. Just as we tumbled in we heard
the Sounds arrive back.

4
An awful lot of pony

THE farrier refused to shoe the next four ponies until he got paid for the first five. Captain Sound grumbled like mad, but he finally paid up, and then said he didn't think he'd have the other four shod after all as it was all going to cost such a lot.

I told him that I thought he'd got too many ponies on his plate anyway. They were going to be an awful expense, and why not just concentrate on getting the five best ones into good shape?

'What about the other four?' he said.

Ann said, seeing that he'd bought the whole lot so cheaply, why not turn the other four loose in the forest again to join the herd before they got civilized?

He thought this over and then decided it was the right thing to do, so one bright morning Ann and I made a string of the four wilder ponies and led them off into the forest. As soon as we got into the glades they began to snuff the air of home and looked gay and happy.

'Okay, girls and boys,' I said. 'You're going home and good luck to you.'

Soon we saw a small herd cropping grass under the ancient trees where as you know, or ought to know, the ancient kings of England used to hunt, and William Rufus or somebody got shot by an arrow by mistake.

We loosed the four ponies and drew back to see what they'd do. They didn't hesitate, they just gave a little prance and trotted off to the others. There was a bit of nuzzling and a bit of neighing – doubtless the four were telling the others about their adventures on the brink of civilization, so to speak – and off they all ran together.

'Golly!' said Ann, 'I wish we'd brought all nine,' and we both began to giggle.

We had both had letters from our mothers that morning. Mummy had written, 'You really didn't say very much in your letter. What is the house like? Are you being well fed? And you don't say a thing about Captain and Mrs Sound. I couldn't care less about Webster's the grocers, so why drag that in?'

Ann's mother said much the same.

Ann groaned. 'Now I've got to concoct another diplomatic letter.'

'Oh,' I said, 'I'm just going to tell them that the Sounds are a little odd, but we're enjoying ourselves.'

So we drew a lot of funny pictures to show how we were enjoying ourselves and posted them off.

Captain Sound was very keen now that we should start training the ponies to the saddle, and five seemed very few to manage after all that crowd. By now they were getting to know us, and were quite friendly and manageable. Ann and I could do much more with them than Captain Sound could.

We started off by fastening blankets on their back and got them over the initial stages of not liking it very much. Then little by little we went through the business of the saddle and the bridle and the bit.

If you think this is easy you ought to try it. It takes endless patience, and we worked all day long, first on one pony and then another. The first time I mounted Happy Dawn it was like a rodeo, he put me off about five times. Mustard and Pepper had by now calmed down a lot, and the fifth pony we had named Rainbow because she was a skewbald.

Captain Sound was always very cheerful and seemed to think everything in the garden was lovely, but we weren't so sure.

I said one day, 'I suppose you realize, Captain Sound, that you're going to have an awful lot of expense if you intend to have a riding-school with these ponies? It's going to be spring before they're ready to carry children, and even then I wouldn't trust them with beginners.'

Captain Sound looked a bit blank.

'Also,' I went on, 'you'll have to do something about building a stable for them, a big one. You can't have them out at grass till the spring. They've got to be clipped and groomed and kept clean. When they come in from rides they'll be wet and dirty and they've got to be got ready for next day's use. You'll have to lay in hay and straw and fodder. And harness and tack. At present you've only got two snaffle bridles and two saddles and one of those is coming to bits. It isn't safe. The girth gave way yesterday and Ann came off, and the saddle was under Pepper's stomach. I hope you don't mind me pointing all this out, but you'll need to get cracking on these things before long.'

He was obviously taken aback. You could tell that he didn't know a thing, and hadn't even considered what needed to be done.

'Oh, I don't know –' he said vaguely. 'I hadn't expected to spend a lot of money. Surely –'

'You can't start a riding-school without spending an awful lot of money,' said Ann, 'unless you're lucky enough to have a place with good stabling to start with, and can do all the work on the ponies yourself, and buy some really sound secondhand tack and saddlery.'

'Oh well,' he said, 'having gone so far I don't see why we should meet our difficulties halfway.'

'He really has got hopeless ideas,' I said, when we

were in our room that night. 'I don't know what's going to happen when the weather turns bad. It's all right now in September but what about December?'

'I don't see why we should worry about the future for him if he can't be bothered to worry himself. Gosh, we're practically doing the housekeeping for Mrs Sound in any case,' said Ann.

This was true. We had taken to doing the shopping and ordering the food ourselves, in self-defence, and one or other of us usually did the cooking too, it was the only way to get anything to eat. Mrs Sound was awfully grateful and thought we were marvellous, but that didn't get us anywhere.

However, a month went by, and it happened to be a gorgeous sunny October, which didn't encourage Captain Sound to make any provision for the winter. By now we really were getting the five ponies into shape by sheer hard work. We worked from about eight in the morning until it was dark, taking one pony in turn and working on it, not tiring it, but being patient and gentle and encouraging the pony's natural sense of fun so that it really enjoyed its training; then going on to another.

Each one of them would now let us ride it, and we would go out on the common with a pair of them, along with my two ponies. The novice ponies seemed to enjoy watching Black Boy and Rapide, and it helped a lot. Happy Dawn and Rapide got along particularly well together, and I would ride first one and then the other. Merry Night had always picked his feet up nicely, and Ann had got him quite well controlled and doing a pretty walk. It was very hard work but we felt it was worth while to see how the ponies were coming along because of our efforts. Mustard and Pepper both had too much sense of humour to be predictable, and were apt to get crazy. They could be very good if they liked, and they could also be terrible. Rainbow was actually the most docile of the five, but she wasn't very bright and was hard to teach, and she had the awful fault of rearing when she thought she had had enough.

Actually we couldn't see any of the five except Happy Dawn and Merry Night being any good in a riding-school, but it was no good saying so to Captain Sound who didn't seem to like to hear common sense.

'After all,' I said to Ann, 'we're not paid to worry about the future.'

'Paid?' she said. 'Who's paid?'

'Gosh, yes,' I said. 'That's another thing.'

We had now been at Little Chimneys Farm for four weeks and nothing had yet been said about our wages, and we hadn't liked to ask.

'I'm going to ask him,' said Ann. 'You know

what he is, he never thinks of anything unless he's prodded.'

So that evening while we were having supper, Ann said, 'By the way, I hope you don't mind me mentioning it, Captain Sound, but we haven't got any money left, and we haven't had our wages yet.'

'Oh I say!' he said. 'It just slipped my mind. I'll give it to you after supper. Thanks for reminding me.'

Mrs Sound cleared away the supper things, and our employer carefully laid down twelve pound notes on the table and said, 'There you are.'

Ann and I stared.

'There's something wrong here,' I said. 'We've been here a month.'

'Well, yes,' he said. 'I've deducted a pound a week for your ponies' keep.'

'But my ponies are out at grass all day!' I said. 'And they get the same as the other ponies every night, and jolly few oats. And if it comes to that, my ponies are working for you all the time. We couldn't have done much without them.'

He thought for a minute and then said, 'Well, if you insist,' and put another two pounds down on the table very reluctantly.

'Excuse me,' said Ann, 'but that's only fourteen pounds. We were to have four pounds a week each.'

'Oh no,' said Captain Sound. 'Four pounds between you.'

Ann and I were furious. Seven pounds each for a whole month's hard work and no square meals! We weren't mercenary, but this was just meanness.

We discussed it in our room, as we were getting into bed.

'I'll tell you what,' said Ann. 'We're leaving. That'll shake him. I don't see how he can do without us.'

'But how on earth can we go home, and tell everybody how we've been done?' I said. 'Our very first job too, that we got for ourselves. They'll think we can't look after ourselves, and they'll never let us do anything again. It'll be domestic science for ever and ever.'

'I don't care,' said Ann. 'Either he gives us the other sixteen pounds tomorrow, or we're leaving.'

'Well, I care,' I said. 'I've got pride. I'm not going home beaten, I'd rather starve to death in the snow.'

'That's what we'll both do if we stay here,' said Ann.

In the middle of arguing we fell asleep.

When we got up next morning we still didn't know what to do, but as we entered the living-room for breakfast Captain Sound came rushing in at the door.

'Where are the ponies?' he shrieked.

We stared.

'What have you done with the ponies?' he said.

'We haven't done anything with them,' I said. 'We fed them as usual last night and left them in the paddock.'

'You left the gate wide open,' he said. 'They've gone.'

'We did not leave the gate open,' said Ann. 'We've never done such a thing. People with our experience don't leave gates open. Actually I distinctly remember fastening it, because I caught my sleeve on the splintered bit on the top.'

'Yes, that's true,' I said.

'Well then, you didn't fasten it properly,' he said.

'Yes we did,' I said. 'We always look to see if the gate is perfectly fast before we leave it. We've had that sort of training.'

He went on blaming us, and we were furious. Just then Mrs Sound came in with the boiled eggs and asked what was the matter.

When she was told she said, 'But you went down to the field yourself last night, George, after the girls had gone to bed. You took the torch, because you said you'd left your jacket on the hedge.'

Captain Sound went scarlet, realizing that it was he who hadn't fastened the gate. He shrugged his shoulders and said, 'Well, that's neither here nor there. The ponies have got out and they've probably been gone for hours. When you've finished your breakfast you'd better go and look for them.'

'This is it,' said Ann, as we rode out half an hour later on my two ponies. 'The ponies have had a jolly good start. If you ask me, they're all back in their native wilds by now.'

First we made for the Common, thinking there was a possibility that the ponies might have settled down to crop grass there, but no. We asked in the village, and a man told us that he'd heard a number of ponies clattering madly down the street in the middle of the night.

'At the rate they were going,' he said, 'they're miles away by now, well out in the Forest. You haven't a hope.'

As you know, the New Forest is enormous. We rode about all the morning and saw plenty of ponies, but none of ours. It was like looking for five needles in a haystack as big as a cinema. Once back in those remote glades the ponies would joyfully decide that they'd had enough civilization to last them for the rest of their lives.

We searched on until we were ready to drop, and finally turned into Lyndhurst at four o'clock and went into a café to get some sandwiches and tea.

It looks to me,' I said, 'as if your comic job has packed up on us without any effort on our part. So what now? We just leave and go home.'

'Can't say I like that,' said Ann. 'Our first job

that we've found for ourselves folding up like this, and we arrive home after one month – after all we've said about being independent. There'll be an awful lot of I-told-you-so.'

'But it isn't our fault.'

'Well, what are we going to tell them? That all the ponies ran away and we couldn't find them, so we gave up and came home? It sounds jolly fishy to me, and it will to all our friends.'

I said I couldn't see how a horsy story could sound fishy, and Ann said, 'Oh, don't be so difficult!' and we started squabbling because we were so fed up.

'Obviously,' I said gloomily, 'we shan't be staying on with the Sounds, so what do we do? If only we could find ourselves another job, and not have to go home in igno-what-do-they-call-it! Perhaps Captain Sound would give us some frightfully good references. He ought to, after all the work we've put in.'

'Work!' said Ann. 'I'm still black and blue with falling off Mustard until I got him to stop bucking. But I'm glad for the ponies' own sakes that they're gone, because I think they'd have had rather a miserable life – the Sounds hadn't a clue how to look after them – and we wouldn't have stuck it there for ever.'

5
The new idea

SUDDENLY a woman at the next table said, 'Excuse me, but did I hear you say you'd been working for Captain Sound? You must be the two girls I've heard about. What happened?'

She looked nice, and soon we had given her a short outline of our story.

'Oh dear,' she said. 'How hopeless. I agree with you, the ponies will never be found, and a good thing too. I don't know what would have happened to the poor things in the end, because the Sounds are hopelessly impractical people and always going in for wonderful-sounding schemes without any knowledge whatever. I know all about them, and this idea of a riding-school was ridiculous from the beginning. I'm only sorry that you too got let in. We know all about you in the neighbourhood, and how good you've been – these things get round – and there certainly wasn't any future there for you. I'm jolly glad I've come across you. What do you propose to do now?'

'I suppose we'll just leave,' said Ann. 'We were going to, anyway.'

'And we'll be out of a job,' I said drearily. 'We'll have to go home, and it'll be an awful let-down, because we were so keen on getting our own pony job and being successful.'

'Would you want another job?' she asked. 'By the way, my name's Mrs York and I live at Pockett House, not far from where you've come from.'

'How do you do?' we said politely, and I added, 'I'm Jill Crewe and this is Ann Derry. We'd love to have another job, as long as it's the kind we like. We don't want another flop.'

'Listen,' said Mrs York, 'I may be able to help you. Could you come along to my house tomorrow and have tea? Anybody in the district will tell you where it is. I've got an idea which I'll explain to you when you come, and if you don't like it there's no harm done. What about it?'

Our spirits rose, and we said we'd come like a shot. It really sounded like a fairy tale where something always turns up just when you think that All Is Lost.

We rode back to Little Chimneys Farm, and reported to Captain Sound that it was everybody's opinion that the ponies would never be found, now that they had succeeded in getting back to the wilds.

He looked very gloomy and said, 'All that money just thrown away!'

We felt like saying, 'All what money?' but felt it

might be cruel to mock him in his Hour of Despair, so we didn't say anything except that now the job had packed up, we'd be packing up too.

At this he went rather red and said we'd helped a lot and been jolly good, and if it hadn't been for the Fell Hand of Fate robbing him of the ponies like that he was sure we'd soon have had a smashing riding-school going, and if he could think of something else perhaps we'd some day come back and help him with it because he thought we were absolutely terrifically good and very hard workers.

I could see the words, 'What About Our Sixteen Pounds?' jumping up and down in Ann's throat, but she swallowed them down. After all, we had our pride and we weren't mercenary people.

Then Mrs Sound said, 'I've never liked anybody so much as Amy and Judy in my life, and it'll be awful to have to start doing the food again,' and practically wept, I mean she sniffed a lot and grabbed her handkerchief.

I tried to keep up the tone of the party by saying, 'Well, all good things come to an end,' but the whole evening was a bit dim.

In case any of you are wondering, none of the ponies ever appeared again, and somewhere in the New Forest there are five ponies called Happy Dawn, Merry Night, Mustard, Pepper, and Rainbow, who will have shed their shoes long, long ago.

If you are ever around that way and notice a very mauve one, that'll be Happy Dawn, and he'll have forgotten everything he ever learned by now.

The next morning we packed our things, and in the afternoon we set off on my two ponies for Pockett House. It turned out to be a huge red brick house with parkland all round it, and Black Boy and Rapide pricked up their ears at the sight of it and were all set for a gallop.

Mrs York saw us from the front window and came running out. She had a round face like the man in the moon and rather odd clothes consisting of a skirt, jumper, and cardigan, none of which remotely matched, but she was awfully kind.

'What adorable ponies!' she said. 'Are they yours?'

'They're Jill's,' said Ann.

'And wherever I go, they go,' I said firmly, so that she'd get the right idea at the start.

'They look to me as if they'd like a good canter round the park,' said Mrs York. 'Well, we'll have to see about that. Now do come in!'

She took us into an enormous drawing-room, with trestle tables in it, and sewing machines, and bits of sewing and knitting all over the place.

'I've had a working party here all morning,' she explained rather unnecessarily, 'and I simply haven't had time to clear up, in fact I hardly ever do, it doesn't seem worth while. Now what do you two girls say to some tea before we do anything else?'

We tried to look polite and not too eager, but I suppose our eyes glittered like the red eyes of famished wolves, as actually all we had had for lunch was a boiled egg each and a sardine between us.

'You look to me,' said Mrs York, 'as if you'd enjoy an enormous tea. I know I would, as I didn't have time for much lunch. 'I've a feeling you didn't get exactly what I'd call lavish meals at the Sounds', Mrs Sound has a reputation for being a bit forgetful.'

'She forgets practically every meal,' said Ann. 'We started doing the catering in self defence, but when we hadn't time nothing happened at all.'

'Good-oh!' said Mrs York. 'Let's have a terrific tea.'

She went out, and in about ten minutes came back followed by a beaming West Indian maid, both of them carrying trays with piles of piping hot buttered crumpets, sandwiches, and cakes, and even little sausages on sticks.

'Now get into that,' said Mrs York, 'and at the same time perhaps you'd like to tell me your life stories.'

We always enjoyed telling our life stories, so for the next half-hour we talked and ate like mad.

'And on top of all that,' said Ann, 'it does seem

jolly hard luck that in our first job we should get all washed up. Of course we'll try and make our mothers and friends realize that Captain Sound wasn't very clever and he was the one who let the ponies escape, so that it won't sound in any way our fault, but I know what they'll say – "you'd better stay at home and do something sensible". Nothing's sensible without ponies.'

'So this is where I come in,' said Mrs York. 'I like you two girls very much, and I think I can help you and give you some fun while you do me a favour in return. Are you interested?'

'Rather!' we said, all agog.

'Well now,' said Mrs York, 'I'm getting up a big bazaar in aid of the refugees. The bazaar is going to be held in this house next month. There are a lot of people in this district who ride, and I thought we could bring them into the affair by organizing a treasure hunt and musical rides. They will all pay to enter, and the musical ride is something that everybody can go out into the park to watch, while the treasure hunt will cause a lot of interest and fun. If it had been summer I would have had a gymkhana, but it isn't summer and I think the two events I've mentioned will be suitable for the autumn weather. My idea is that you two girls come here and stay with me as my guests, and organize the two events. What do you think about that?'

'It sounds gorgeous to me,' I said.

'Me too,' said Ann. 'What should we have to do?'

'Have you ever organized anything of the kind before?' asked Mrs York.

We told her that we had organized pretty well every kind of event in the pony world.

'I shall want you to go round and visit all the people who ride,' said Mrs York, 'and get them to enter, and collect their entrance fee – say fifteen pence each –'

'Twenty-five,' I suggested. 'Don't make it too cheap. They'll all pay twenty-five pence for so much fun, and I suppose there'll be prizes for the treasure hunt?'

'Oh yes, that's another thing. I'd like you to persuade the local tradespeople to give some prizes. And you'll have to make a list of things for the treasure hunt itself and train people for the musical ride, and take all that off my hands.'

We thought for a minute and then nodded at each other, having decided that this seemed just our kind of job.

'There's one thing, Mrs York,' I said. 'Shall I be able to keep my two ponies here?'

'Oh, but of course!' she said. 'That's no problem. We've got plenty of stabling at the farm and four horses of our own. The ponies will be useful to you, so count them in as our guests too. And by the way, I have a girl staying here just about your age, my god-daughter, who's helping me with the bazaar, so you'll have young company. Now when can you come?'

'We've only got to move out,' said Ann, 'so we could come tomorrow morning if you like.'

'Splendid,' said Mrs York. 'Now I know you're going to enjoy yourselves here. Work that's fun and fun that's work, and plenty of both, has always been my motto. Perhaps you'd like to see the room you'll have?'

She took us upstairs and showed us a very large bedroom with two beds and windows that looked over the park. Although there was plenty of furniture in it, there still looked enough space to give a party, very different from our cramped quarters at the Sounds'.

'It seems an absolutely smashing set-up,' I said to Ann as we trotted down the drive. 'Do you think there's a snag in it?'

'Oh, don't let's be gruesome,' she said. 'Mrs York seems a jolly nice person and at least she isn't scatty! I'm just wondering what we're going to say when we write home. Mummy may go off the deep end about me finding myself a job with a complete stranger.'

'Well, let's get settled in before we write,' I suggested, 'and then we can tell our mothers how nice it is and they'll be appeased. Isn't it marvellous that we haven't to go home after all?'

Next morning we said farewell to the Sounds. To our surprise Captain Sound had a complete change of heart and pressed the missing sixteen pounds into our hands, and Mrs Sound really cried, and said, 'Good-bye, my darling Amy and Judy,' and presented us each with a half-pound carton of chocolates, so they really weren't so bad after all.

We rode to Pockett House, and the first thing Mrs York did was to take us down to the farm where my ponies were going to be stabled.

I was absolutely thrilled with it.

The whole place was most beautifully kept, and the farmer couldn't have been pleasanter. He showed us the stalls he had got ready for Black Boy and Rapide, and they took to him at once and started nuzzling his shoulder and whiffling at his hands, because they could tell he loved horses, so I felt very happy.

The floor of their stalls was of red brick laid in a herringbone pattern, and next door were the corn bins and running water, and there was a harness room for my tack, and a barn filled with hay and straw. It was a marvellous place. The other four horses on the farm consisted of three working horses, and a pony thirty years old which had been ridden by Mrs York in her youth, and was now enjoying its old age in perfect bliss.

Ann and I stayed among all these horses for ages, having the time of our lives until I realized it was nearly one o'clock and we ought to be getting back to the house. We went in at a side door and there was a lovely smell of lunch.

'Well, what did you think of the place?' asked Mrs York.

'Smashing,' I said. 'It's just the sort of farm I'd like to have myself some day. I could stay there all day. Is it all right for us to ride in the park when we're off duty?'

'Of course,' said Mrs York. 'That's where you'll have to arrange your practices for the musical ride. I suppose you've seen one done?'

I said we'd both seen one at the Olympic Tattoo on television, and had got the general idea.

Mrs York told us to go into the morning-room, and lunch would be ready in five minutes. We washed first in a handy little cloakroom, and then went and stood warming ourselves in front of a gorgeous fire in the morning-room which was panelled in dark oak and had window-seats.

Presently the door opened, and a girl came in.

'Now!' cried Mrs York. 'Here's my god-daughter who is dying to get to know you.'

I looked round.

'I bet she is!' I said sarkily, and Ann said, 'Oh golly!'

Mrs York's god-daughter was my cousin Cecilia.

6
It's Cecilia

THOSE of you who have read my previous books will know all about the ancient feud which had been waged between my cousin Cecilia and myself from my earliest years.

When I was young she was always held before me as the kind of model I ought to build myself up to, so to speak. Cecilia was never dirty, she was never rough, she never said Oh Gosh or Blast or Sucks to you. She never yelled or got furious or broke cups or left the electric light on or lost her handkerchiefs or spilt ink or was late for school or couldn't find her atlas.

Cecilia, I had been told from my infancy, knitted beautifully from about the age of five, and passed the cups when her mother had people to tea without sloshing the tea into the saucers, and always wrote at once to thank people for things they'd given her. She also went to the dentist when she had to, without making a fuss.

Our mothers being sisters, I suppose they had always had a beautiful dream of Cecilia and me being loving friends, but what a hope! I had been to stay with Cecilia and Cecilia had been to stay with me. These visits had hardly been a howling success. Cecilia was a completely unhorsy person, and yet she pretended to know more about horses than I did. She was an awful show-off. She never read anything but books called *The Madcap of the Lower Fourth*, and so on. And she was a shocking fusser. I've known Cecilia wreck a whole picnic just because one wasp came buzzing around her plate, and everybody knows that if you don't bother a wasp it won't bother you, but if you get it excited what can you expect?

Oh well, I suppose there had to be a snag at Pockett House, and here it was, all dressed up in a pink tweed skirt and a matching twin set.

'Hullo, Cecilia,' I croaked.

'Jill!' she said. 'I might have known!'

'I say, do you two know each other?' said Mrs York. 'How nice!'

'We're cousins,' I said.

'Only Jill is *so* horsy,' said Cecilia. 'But I should think just the right one for the job, Aunt Pat. She adores dragging ponies about, and backing them into things and so on, and she doesn't mind how wet she gets. And Ann's another the same.'

'Isn't that wonderful?' said Mrs York, quite missing the fact that Cecilia was being sarky. 'Now I'll go and hurry up the lunch.'

As soon as she was gone Cecilia gave a delicate sniff and said, 'Somebody's been around the stables.'

'Our clothes are perfectly clean, if that's what you mean,' I said, 'and we're not going to stand for that sort of remark! You dress like a lampshade if you want to, and if it's suitable to your job, and we'll dress suitably for ours.'

'I'm sure you will,' said Cecilia. 'Jodhpurs from morning till night!'

'Oh, call a truce,' said Ann. 'What sort of a life am I going to have with you two getting at each other all the time?'

'That's all right by me,' I said. 'Live and let live – as long as Cecilia doesn't try to teach me anything about ponies.'

'Oh, I gave up ponies long ago,' said Cecilia airily. 'They're childish.'

'Some poor pony will be relieved,' I said.

At that moment the situation was saved by the lunch bell.

Next morning Ann and I began our duties. The first thing was to get people to enter for the events, so Mrs York gave us a list and we sallied forth.

The first place we called at was a farm, and the farmer's wife said at once, 'Oh yes, mine would all love to join.'

'How many?' I said, and she said five, three girls and two boys.

'I suppose they've all got ponies,' said Ann, and the farmer's wife said that was the snag, they only had one and a half ponies between them, that was to say they had one pony of their own and part-time use of another which belonged to a girl who did part-time book-keeping at the hotel.

'But they're used to sharing,' said the farmer's wife. 'I mean, one gets off and another gets on.'

'I'm afraid that wouldn't be much use in a treasure hunt or a musical ride,' I said. 'What a pity, as we do want people.'

The farmer's wife said that the children might be able to borrow some horses from somewhere on the day, and we said we were afraid that wasn't much good as we wanted to start practices as soon as possible; and the farmer's wife said we could count on one of the children anyway; they'd just have to draw lots for which one, and it was pretty sure to be Josephine as she was born lucky, and we had to leave it at that.

Ann got out the list and wrote Josephine Pobley on the fair white sheet, and that was *one*.

The next place we called at was the doctor's house. As we approached we heard the sweet thunder of hoofs, and in the paddock next to the house a boy and girl were doing a racing gallop.

'Hi!' we shouted.

They pulled up, slid off, and came over to us.

'What do you want?'

We told them about the events and they were very keen.

'Have you ever done a musical ride?' I asked.

'I haven't,' said the boy, 'but I shouldn't think it's hard to learn. Nan was in one once, weren't you, Nan?'

'Yes,' said Nan. 'We got one up in the riding-class and it was the most frightful mess. All the ponies either turned the same way, or crashed into each other. Miss Stocks was livid.'

'Well, that's encouraging, I must say!' I said.

'Oh, it wasn't so bad really,' said Nan. 'It only wanted a bit more organizing. We only had two practices.'

'I'm all for the treasure hunt,' said the boy. 'I've always wanted to be in one.'

'All right,' said Ann, 'we'll stick your names down and we'll let you know when the first practice is.'

They said their names were Nan and Peter Bruce, and the person we ought to go and see was a girl called Dulcie Willow at Fuller's Cottage, as she had some riding pupils and would probably enter them *en bloc*, so to speak.

So we popped off to Fuller's Cottage. My idea of a girl called Dulcie Willow was somebody very fair and swaying and about eighteen, but actually she was very fat and brisk and had a voice like a foghorn, and she was quite old, about twenty-five I should think.

'I don't know who you are, but come on in,' she boomed as we approached the open door; and in we went to find her eating scrambled eggs with a grey pony.

That is to say, Dulcie was sitting at the table eating the eggs, and the pony was standing opposite to her eating cornflakes and bread out of a tin bowl on the table.

'I say,' said Ann, 'does she eat all her meals with you?'

'Of course she does,' said Dulcie. 'She's got better manners and is better company than most people I know. Who are you and what can I do for you?'

I told her that we were staying with Mrs York who was getting up a bazaar, and our job was to organize some pony events.

'We were told that you had a riding-school and that you'd be just the person to get us some people to enter for the events,' I said.

'If anybody told you I've got a riding-school they're up the pole,' said Dulcie cheerfully. 'I take a few pupils, but I'm jolly particular who I take. I can't do with these Know-All kids, and I haven't the slightest use for people who only want to ride so that they can win things.'

'I couldn't agree more,' I said. 'When you go to gymkhanas nowadays half the people aren't there for fun or good riding but only to win, and they glower at the other competitors and are beastly to their ponies if they lose. My friend and I are only interested in good horsemanship.'

'Then you're the sort of people I like to know,' said Dulcie. 'Pour yourselves some coffee, it's on the gas. I can give you the names of some decent kids for your ride and treasure hunt. Move over, Susannah.'

The pony obligingly moved over, and from a drawer in the table Dulcie took a writing pad and a pencil and began to jot things down, while we took her at her word and helped ourselves to some coffee.

'There's Pamela Shooter,' said Dulcie. 'She's got a pretty pony with lots of sense. What would you say to a palomino? Or do you want the ponies paired, two grey, two chestnut, and so on?'

'I don't think so,' said Ann. 'We don't want it to look too formal. It would be very colourful to have a palomino, and a few piebalds and skewbalds if we can come across them.'

'Rightio,' said Dulcie. 'That'll be John Hicks on his palomino, and – now let me see, who's got a piebald? – oh yes, Janet and Pam Watts on two piebalds, though Janet's an awful person for falling off, and that wouldn't look so good in a musical ride. We'll have to glue her to the saddle or something. You'd better go and see the Fosters. They both ride awfully well and have lovely ponies, and they'll give a lot of tone to your show, but they've got one of those fussy mothers who only likes them to ride in the very best events. You'll have to convince her that yours is one of the very best events.'

'I don't know,' I said. 'I don't feel that I and the Fosters would click.'

'Okay,' she said. 'Wash out the Fosters, but if they come to you of their own accord and ask to enter, have them. Now there's the vicar's son, Noel Shaw, he'll make a leader, but you can't have him without having his brother Tony, and Tony's an absolute clown and always playing for laughs.'

'I say!' said Ann. 'I didn't know there were so many snags in getting up a musical ride.'

'If I were you two,' said Dulcie Willow, 'I'd get all the kids round and try them out, then winkle out the ones you really want for the ride.'

'I don't know if that would do,' I said. 'We need a lot of entries because of the twenty-five pences for the bazaar, and if we hurt people's feelings by telling them they're not good enough they'll sheer off in disgust, and Mrs York will get hardly any money at all.'

'Oh, I don't think you need worry,' boomed Dulcie. 'They can all go in for the treasure hunt, there's no limit. I should hand-pick about sixteen for the ride and take a collection from the spectators.'

'That's an idea,' I agreed. 'Coo, I feel like Napoleon planning a campaign.'

We went round and visited the people whose names she had given us, and a few more, and told them all to turn up the following morning at Pockett House for a practice in the park.

Mrs York was pleased with what we had done, especially when next day she saw the people and the ponies arriving.

I suddenly got cold feet and said, 'Oh help!'

'What's the matter?' said Mrs York.

'I just wondered how all these people would take to being told things by Ann and me, when we're only about their own age and they don't even know us.'

'Oh, I'll go out and make them a speech,' said Mrs York. 'It'll be all right. What are you going to do, Cecilia?'

Cecilia said she would watch us from the window and make tea cosies, or dainty doilies, or something, for the bazaar.

I don't know about Ann, but my knees were knocking together as we went out and faced twenty people with ponies who all stood staring at us in a glazed sort of way.

Mrs York stood on the steps and said, 'I'm so glad all you people have turned up and I'm sure you're going to have fun.' She then introduced Ann and me to them, and said a lot of their names which I felt I hadn't a hope of remembering, and went on, 'Jill and Ann are going to be in charge of the training and organization, so you do as they say. Agreed?'

Nobody seemed to object so Mrs York pushed off and left us to it. The first thing I asked was whether anybody had ever done a musical ride before. Blank silence. Ann said, 'Has anybody ever seen a musical ride?' and about twelve put their hands up, and one boy said, 'On television and it looks jolly easy.'

'That's what you think!' I said.

A girl said, 'It's possible if you're a competent rider, but some people hardly know their left rein from their right, and the music puts you off a bit, anyway.'

'Well, let's have a shot without any music, because we haven't got any yet,' I said. 'All get into line and walk a circle, and I'll watch your performance and see how the ponies match up.'

Although it was early November it was a lovely, mild, sunny day and the grass was sparkling and the sky blue. As soon as the ponies began to walk round I felt fine. It was a wonderful feeling, as only horsy people can understand.

'Do we match the colours of the ponies?' said Ann. 'Or do we mix them up?'

I said I didn't see how we could attempt to match the colours, or the heights and comparative performances would be all wrong, so we'd study the performance first and then see how the heights went.

The performances were, needless to say, pretty mixed. A few people were good, experienced riders, and a few looked as if they had been in the saddle about three times in their whole lives.

'Gosh!' I muttered to Ann. 'This'll take some sorting out.' As I said it, one girl fell off for no apparent reason at all and her pony went lolloping away across the park. Everybody stopped while the girl chased her pony, and when she got back another girl called Althea Something said she was bored stiff already, and in any case we'd have to pick out the best people for the leaders and it was obvious who the best people were.

'Noel Shaw and I had better be the leaders,' she said. 'Our ponies are the same height and have much the same pace.'

Several people began to mutter at this, and a girl said, 'It isn't fair. Althea and Noel seem to think they have to lead everything. Why can't Judy and I lead? We're as good as they are.'

'Don't be silly,' said Althea. 'You're too little and fat to lead anything, and Judy rides on the rein all the time. That's no example to people.'

Judy started shrieking at this, and I said, 'I haven't seen enough of any of you to decide anything yet. I'm going to pair you off myself, on performance, and we'll see what happens.'

I felt that Althea wanted taking down a peg, so I picked out a quiet-looking boy and girl for the leading pair and followed them up with Althea and Noel, and Judy and the little fat girl who was called Lucille. Eventually Ann and I arranged the ten pairs, but the grumbling nearly shook the leaves off the trees, people saying that they couldn't possibly ride with the people I had partnered them with.

'All right!' I yelled, 'It's only temporary, can't you grasp that? I've got to make a start somewhere.'

At last I got the pairs riding round, and it was obvious that the leaders I had chosen were a bit too quiet, and very slow, and held up the rest.

'There you are,' said Althea. 'You'll have to let me and Noel lead after all.'

I was afraid she was right, so we tried it that way, but the spacing proved frightful as the leaders rode much too fast for the pair behind, and the third pair crowded the second, and so on right down the line.

I told them that they simply must keep an equal distance apart, and some managed this and some didn't.

'It's having all these inexperienced kids in,' said Tony Shaw in disgust. 'We shall look a motley gang, with a few good riders in front and a trail of hopeless kids behind.'

'Don't worry,' I said coldly. 'The kids will probably be better than you when I've done with them. In any case I shall put a good pair at the end to finish the team off.'

'Well, I hope it won't be Alec and me,' said the boy.

'It'll be the ones I decide it will be,' I said.

Meanwhile Ann was changing a few people's places, and then we tried them again and it was a bit better.

'I'm bored with this already,' said Althea. 'It's going to be pretty dull just forming twos and fours and eights when I could do it without any practice at all. I don't think I'll come any more.'

I could see the musical ride falling to bits if I wasn't careful.

'Oh, be a sport,' I said. 'People will be paying to watch you ride on the day, and it's all in aid of the refugees, and we can't have it at all if the best riders won't take part.'

'That's right,' said Noel, unexpectedly coming to my aid. 'I think we jolly well ought to do it, Althea.'

'That's right,' I said. 'Somebody back us up. It's all in a good cause, and I think you might try a bit harder. Look, Ann and I will do a demonstration.'

So Ann and I rode up in single file, and at the top I turned left and Ann turned right. Then we rode up as a pair and turned left.

'There you are,' I said. 'And surely the second pair can remember to turn right. Just *try*.'

After that it was a bit better, though some people like Tony Shaw – whom I could cheerfully have murdered – thought they were there to act the fool and clown about. There always are some people like this, I don't know why. I hope nobody who reads this book is one.

At last we decided they'd had enough for one day and sent them off home. A few said they'd enjoyed it, and some didn't say anything at all. I was beginning to wonder whether, after all, this wasn't going to be as bad as training New Forest ponies.

7
Wasn't it murder?

'PHEW!' said Ann. 'Wasn't it murder?'

I said I was sure the thing would sort itself out when the people got more used to us, and to riding in formation with each other, and Ann said she jolly well hoped I was right.

'You certainly worked hard,' said Mrs York, 'and some of them didn't seem very helpful.'

'The whole point is,' I said, 'that they're not getting much out of it except hard work and being bossed around. Althea was right, it isn't much fun for them, they'd be far happier having a country ride or practising something they enjoy doing. Some of the older ones are prepared to do it to be sporting, but others just aren't as sporting as all that!'

'And they've got to groom their ponies and come out here on their school's free afternoon and Saturday morning,' said Ann. 'I feel as if we'd got to offer more inducement or they'll just fade away.'

Mrs York looked quite upset and said, 'You're right! I ought to have thought, and now I feel awful about it. I let them go off this afternoon without even offering them a biscuit and a drink of pop, and if they never come any more it's my fault.'

'Oh don't worry,' I said. 'They couldn't be as unsporting as that.'

'Jill seems to think everybody ought to be so sporting!' said Cecilia. 'Oh, these horsy people!'

'Well, you're not one, so kindly keep out of it,' I said, in my sweet, cousinly way, and Mrs York looked a bit shaken.

However she recovered and said, 'In future I'll see to it that they get cokes and cakes whenever they come, and of course there will be a present for everybody who takes part in the ride on the day.'

'Goody!' said Ann. 'We'll tell them that.'

'Really?' said Cecilia. 'Fancy having to bribe people!'

'Oh shut up,' said Ann, who also knew what Cecilia was like. By now Mrs York looked quite agitated, and to stop her from going into a complete flap Ann and I went on talking hurriedly about our team until gradually she got interested and calmed down.

At the next practice, four of our original twenty didn't turn up, the boy called Alec and his partner Tony Shaw, the girl who had fallen off her pony, and one of the younger kids, and when we asked about them it appeared that Alec and Tony didn't want to come any more as they thought it silly, and the mother of the girl who had fallen off wouldn't let her come any more because she said it was dangerous, and the small kid had got measles.

'None of the other sixteen must fall out,' I said, 'or we shan't have a team. We'll have to butter them up a bit.'

'Team or no team,' said Ann, 'I'm not taking anything from that bossy Althea.'

However, Althea ceased to be bossy and was quite pleasant when it was finally decided that she and Noel should be the leaders. Nan and Peter Bruce were also very good, and so were Pamela Shooter and her partner, and we started matching the rest of the people for ponies and height. Judy and Lucille yelled like mad when we separated them, but we had to convince them that they looked hopeless together, and at last they agreed to ride with other partners. Judy settled for Janet Watts because she liked Janet's piebald, and Lucille said, 'In that case I'll have John Hicks because I want to ride with his palomino,' and John said, 'Oh help, I want to ride with another boy!'

'Oh come on, John, be a sport,' I said. 'At this rate we'll never get matched up,' and to my relief he said okay.

The coke and cakes arriving at that moment brightened things up quite a lot.

Fortified by this, we thought we would have a go at the actual ride. Most of you must have seen a musical ride, and our idea was quite simple, everybody to ride up in single file, the ponies to turn left and right alternately, then up in pairs, left and right again, up in fours, and eights, and finally the whole sixteen abreast.

We marked out a sort of arena with poles, and hauled the sixteen riders into position and set them off. They were supposed to keep a pony length apart, but of course this didn't happen, the first few were all right but after that there was chaos.

'Walk, Janet!' I shouted. 'Don't trot.'

'Breeze won't walk,' Janet shrieked. 'She's fed up with walking, she wants to trot.'

'My Russian rabbits!' said Noel Shaw, turning round. 'Hasn't the girl got any control over her pony?'

'You look after your own pony,' I said, 'and never mind what's going on behind you.'

'It sounds like a stampede going on behind me,' said Noel.

'Use your legs!' shouted Ann. 'We've got to have a balanced pace.'

'Oh, let's try the turns,' I suggested, 'and look after the pace later.'

The ragged file rode on, one or two excited ponies dancing sideways, and others trying to pass the one in front. Indignant remarks flew through the air.

'Never mind!' I shouted. 'Come on up the centre. First pony left, second pony right.'

The first four ponies, ridden by Althea, Noel, Nan, and Peter, did it correctly, but Janet Watts instead of turning left followed Peter to the right and after that it was wild confusion.

'Get yourselves sorted out,' I said. 'We'll have to go on doing this until you get it right.'

We tried again and things improved, until one child's pony at the back suddenly broke into a smart canter, careered past all the rest, and went galloping across the park. The child shrieked, four people set off in pursuit, and the pony finally came to a stop with his saddle under his tummy and the child clinging upside down under his neck. It looked so funny that everybody burst out laughing, and strangely enough it put everybody into a good temper and they did better after that.

Next we tried the pairs, and of course there were any amount of collisions.

'Oi!' shouted John Hicks. 'When my partner gets ahead do I keep my place or keep up with her?'

'Keep your place,' said Ann, 'and Lucille, you *must* keep the right length whatever happens.'

Lucille grumbled, 'That's not very easy when people behind are shoving into you.'

In the end Ann went and fetched Black Boy and Rapide and she and I rode alongside the most feeble ones and showed them, and pushed them, and even hauled them about.

'Crumbs!' I said. 'Wouldn't you think it would be simple to watch the pair in front and just turn the opposite way?'

'Well, it isn't,' said a girl called Cherry Johnson, 'because the people in front start turning one way and then realize they're wrong and turn the other way, and by then you're up the pole.'

So Ann and I rode with each pair in turn and at last we got them straightened out. By the time we got the twos into fours the turning was simplified, but we could not get the person on the inside to pivot while the one on the outside took the wide turn, and the place looked like a battlefield.

'Somebody said this would be easy!' I said bitterly.

'I did,' said Noel, 'and so it would be if we didn't have to cope with all these beginners.'

'Don't exaggerate,' said Ann, 'even if they're not all as clever as you. I'll tell you what, let's get the music out and see what happens. It'll make things more fun.'

Mrs York and the gardener brought out the enormous record player, and we put on a march and turned it up to full strength. The effect on the ponies was atomic. The few who were used to hearing bands at shows didn't bother, but the others went mad, bucking and prancing, side-stepping and rearing, and soon they were cantering away in all directions, half the riders shrieking, 'Stop, stop!' and the other half yelling with laughter. This brought the practice to an end, and we decided that next time we should have to start off with some nice, soothing music.

'You've no idea how funny you two looked,' said Cecilia when we went in. 'All that pandemonium over a simple thing like a musical ride.'

I could have thought of a few things to say, but instead I walked upstairs with terrific dignity. In my room was an approving letter from Mummy. I had written to tell her that we had left Little Chimneys Farm because all the ponies had got lost and Captain Sound had given up the idea of the riding-school, and that now we were staying with Cecilia's godmother and having a wonderful time. The fact that Cecilia was staying there too seemed to give Mummy a lot of unnecessary joy.

In the afternoon Mrs York took us in the car to Bournemouth to look at the shops and have tea. The shop-window gazing wasn't too successful, as Ann and I couldn't find a horsy shop so decided we wanted to look at horsy books in a bookshop, while Cecilia wanted to get some new ideas for tea-cosies at an arty-crafty shop, and we were all so frightfully polite and self-sacrificing to impress Mrs York that we nearly blew up.

The tea, however, put us all in a good humour. It

was supersonic. While Mrs York was paying the bill we decided that we'd like to buy her a present, so Ann and I being very noble said that Cecilia could choose it, and we each gave her fifteen pence, and she went off into the department store where the café was. But when she came back we realized we had been a bit too noble, as what she had bought was a chiffon square in washy mauve with peculiar brown cacti printed on it. While wondering how we should apologize for it, we realized that Mrs York was gushing over with thanks and admiration, and she promptly tied it round her neck and wore it all the way home, looking horrid. She never had it off after that, and Cecilia looked smug, and Ann and I were able to answer the question we had often asked ourselves, Who buys all the gruesome things in shops we feel sick to look at?

Mrs York then decided that it would be a good thing if we went round and asked a few people to give us prizes, as we should need a lot for the bazaar competitions and the treasure hunt.

We felt a bit dim about this, as it was hardly in our line and we weren't very good at asking people for things.

'I'm sure Cecilia will go with you,' said Mrs York. Our eyes nearly popped out with horror, we felt that would be the last straw, but Cecilia was all for it; and, surprisingly, we were soon glad we had taken her because she proved to be a wizard at getting things out of people. You would think she had been doing it all her life, in fact she probably had.

We sailed into the grocer's shop where Mrs York dealt, and Cecilia began to make a lovely speech all about The Cause, etc., and the grocer fell for it like one o'clock and promised Cecilia some tins of chocolate biscuits.

Then we went into the draper's and out came Cecilia's little speech again, and the draper was practically weeping with emotion as he promised some boxes of handkerchiefs. At the confectioner's we landed two iced cakes, and at the china shop some glass dishes and ash trays, and at the fancy shop some arty calendars and wooden owls with pencils through their noses.

So it went on, everybody falling over themselves to promise masses of prizes. Quite honestly, Cecilia had done it, we had hardly said a word.

'There!' she said. 'That's how it's done. Of course you have to have the right manner, and somehow horsy people never do.'

Ann and I could have slain her, but on the other hand she had done our job for us in a terrific way, which proved that everybody is good for something, even a person like Cecilia; and Mrs York was so excited at the forty-seven prizes we had amassed that she praised us like mad, and I must say Cecilia was sporting enough not to say that she'd done it all herself.

Ann and I were now back at the game of struggling with the musical ride.

'The trouble,' said Cecilia, giving us her unasked advice, 'is that half those kids can't really ride. The onlooker sees most of the game.'

Ann said it was a pity that the onlooker was so clever as to keep one eye on the game and the other on the tea-cosy, and the onlooker would soon be developing a squint and dropping a few stitches, and I said sarkily that perhaps the onlooker would like to do the training herself?

'Nothing simpler,' said Cecilia. We gasped.

'Done!' said Ann. 'You flipping well take them this afternoon.'

Without turning a hair Cecilia said it was a bore but she'd show us for once, and we said okay get on with it, and she said, thanks I will, and we said good luck to you, and she said don't mention it.

So when the sixteen riders arrived that afternoon – and very glad we were to see sixteen, because we wouldn't have been surprised if about eight had fallen out and we would have found ourselves with no ride, no nothing – instead of Us greeting them, there stood Cecilia in her pink jumper and skirt, and lipstick on, and believe or believe me not, they all looked at her as if she was the crowned queen of Hickstead. There wasn't a grumble out of any of them, they were so impressed, and Cecilia twiddled her pearl beads – yes, she actually had some on – and said, 'Heads up, knees up, and hands down, and when I say it I mean it, and keep like that; and ride with your knees and not your reins, and if I see anybody sawing at the reins they'll get sent off, and if anybody but ME says anything *they'll* get sent off too.'

Ann and I wouldn't have dared to talk to them like that in case any of them did go off, but they took it from Cecilia. She got them into pairs, and two, not one, pony lengths between each pair, and then said, '*Now* don't tell me you can't see what the pair in front are going to do!'

She bossed them like I've never in my life heard anybody bossed, and they took it! They rode in a silence that was uncanny, and even the kids at the back did it right.

Cecilia said, 'We'd better have somebody good to bring up the rear or it'll look like a sick snake,' and she ordered Nan and Peter to go to the back.

They went without a mutter. If I'd told them there'd have been a scene.

When she had put the team through the whole performance – singles, pairs, fours, eights, and finally the whole sixteen – Cecilia calmly said, 'You can have your break now,' and while they were clustering round Mrs York's tray of cakes she walked over to Ann and me, still twiddling her pearl beads, and said, 'There you are – positively easy.'

We hadn't a word to say. Cecilia strolled into the house and left us to carry on. Humiliating as it sounds, from that moment we had hardly any trouble with the team. We couldn't understand what had happened until we heard that a story was going round the village that the girl in pink was really Ann Moore! I mean – Cecilia! And all she actually knew about riding was what I had managed to din into her when she was staying at my home.

8
Brushing up the team

'WHAT dear Cecilia didn't take the trouble to notice,' said Ann, 'is that only about four people out of the sixteen know how to put on a pony's tack. What with tight girths and loose bits it's a disgusting sight. Do you think we dare tell them?'

I giggled. 'They'll probably appeal to Cecilia if we do. Let's say we're going to have a tack inspection.'

We made everybody stand by his or her pony's head, and went round the lot. Hardly a buckle was right, and by the time that Ann and I had slackened or tightened the lot we never wanted to see a buckle again and were thoroughly unpopular, except with Althea, Noel, and the two Bruces who were very smug when we couldn't find a thing the matter with their ponies.

We made everybody unsaddle, and then we found out the sort of grooming that lazy people do!

'You're a horrid lot,' said Ann. 'What do you think a pony feels like with dirt and sand under the saddle? I'd like to fill all your shoes with grit and make you run in them.'

The people she was referring to looked shame-faced, and Lucille who was one of them said, 'I've only left it once, I was in a hurry so I just groomed the part that shows, but I won't do it again.'

'I should think not,' I said. 'Take your pony round to the farm behind the house and ask them to lend you a dandy brush – and you too, Vincent. And if ever I find a sore or a girth gall on either of your ponies I'll have you eaten alive by my tiger.'

'What tiger?' said Lucille, and I replied, 'The tiger I keep specially for people like you. Leave your saddles here, and bring your ponies back clean.'

The two of them set off at a run, and everybody else laughed, and somebody said, 'They believed you about the tiger.'

'At least you'll all have your tack on properly,' I said. 'Don't the people who teach you tell you this sort of thing?'

Several people hung their heads and muttered that of course they were taught, but since they stopped having regular lessons they hadn't bothered so much, and I said heatedly, 'What do you think you were taught for? So that you'd do things properly for the rest of your life, and be able to show other people, and be a credit to horse-manship. Next time you feel lazy about putting on your tack properly, think of it from the pony's point of view, and think how awful you feel if you've got your coat buttoned in the wrong buttons, or the left shoe on the right foot, or something too tight round your middle.'

'That sunk in all right,' said Ann, as we watched people very carefully checking their tack. 'We could do something about making them sit straighter. I've noticed that they don't all have their stirrup leathers dead straight. Even Noel pushes his back a bit.'

'Well, what's the matter with that?' said Noel when we mentioned it to him. 'I'm used to it.'

'Your seat can't be as firm as it should,' I said. 'You'd find that out if you did any cross-country jumping. Why not get it right once and for all? All the books say that the stirrup leather must be perfectly perpendicular.'

'I'll have a try,' said Noel. 'There, is that right? . . . It feels jolly awkward to me.'

'Get used to it,' I said. 'If your weight is right in the saddle you'll soon feel perfectly balanced. Come a bit further forward – that's better.'

'Yes, it is better,' agreed Noel. 'Thanks for showing me.'

By now everyone was looking down to see if their stirrup leathers were straight and very few were, so they all began to adjust rapidly, and said how weird the correct position made them feel.

'But I expect it's the same as in playing golf,' said Althea. 'When you hold the club properly it feels terrible, but as soon as you realize it's the only way to hit the ball a lovely bash you wonder however you managed to hold it wrong.'

Soon we had them riding in a circle and all the stirrup leathers were dead straight. The difference it made to everybody's appearance was remarkable.

'There'll be sure to be people here on the day,' said Ann, 'who'll make rude remarks about the riding if they get the chance. Don't let's give them the chance.'

'I say,' said Nan Bruce, 'couldn't we do some of that weaving in and out riding?'

'You can try it if you like,' I said, 'but I'm afraid some of the younger ones will get woven into a solid mass.'

They did try it, but it turned out a frightful mess, though it caused a lot of fun and people were good-tempered about it. We decided that we'd better concentrate on getting our ordinary programme perfect. They all had the idea of the simple figures by now and weren't making many mistakes.

'But there hasn't to be one – not one single mistake on the day,' I pointed out, 'because only one would ruin the whole thing.'

'The riding looks very, very much nicer,' said Mrs York when we went in to lunch. 'I don't know an awful lot about it, but they all look smarter somehow.'

Cecilia smirked and said, 'I did my best with them, Aunt Pat.'

Ann and I exchanged glances, and Ann said, 'It's funny, Cecilia, that you didn't notice that half the saddles were too tight and most of the bits practically hanging on the ponies' front teeth, and that everybody's stirrup leathers were at a different angle. Jill and I spent half the morning putting that right, that's why they look better.'

Cecilia said, 'The two kids next to the back looked a scream. They had their tongues hanging out and their hands up nearly under their chins. They looked as if they were begging for biscuits.'

'We were concentrating on legs this morning,' I said in a snooty sort of way. 'We'll see to hands next time.'

Ann giggled, and as we went up to our room she said, 'Cecilia nearly got us that time. I was looking at the legs so hard I honestly never noticed the hands, and evidently you didn't either. Gorgeous sort of teachers we are, I must say!'

Next time the team met we looked hard at the two kids Cecilia had mentioned, and there was a lot in what she said.

'It's Rose and Arthur,' I said. 'They look like two poodles asking to be taken out.'

We thought it was unfair to single out these two

kids, so we made the whole line stop and told everybody to check the position of their hands. Immediately Rose and Arthur went scarlet and brought their hands down with a bump, and then looked round anxiously to see if anybody had noticed.

'That's better,' I said, 'only some people's elbows are now sticking out at the sides. Rose, get your fists out of your tummy and relax your hands. Goodness, Lucille, don't wave your elbows –'

'Are mine all right?' shouted Judy. I told her that her wrists and fingers were too stiff. Eventually I managed to get everybody's hands on a level with the reins, and we did a bit of stopping and starting in that position, some of the lazy ones complaining that it was all a frightful effort, though the more sensible ones realized that it made things easier and the ponies appreciated it.

Unfortunately after this practice the weather broke and we had gales and torrents of rain, so we had to miss several practices. Mrs York was worried in case the day of the bazaar should be bad and the musical ride washed out of existence, and Ann and I were more worried still lest we should have to carry out the ride without sufficient practice and it would be a mess.

Meanwhile we started planning the treasure hunt in which we hoped that practically every rider in the district was going to join.

First we collected a huge number of cocoa tins

and mustard tins and other small tins which had held coffee powder, nutmegs, and so on. Then into each tin we put a slip of paper on which was written either Prize or Bad Luck. There were twenty prizes, and all the other papers were bad luck ones. Then we made a plan of the park and marked the spots where we were going to bury the tins when the weather cleared up, and we wrote out the clues, such as, 'South-south-west of the big chimney stands a tree that looks like a parrot. Find a spot with no moss and dig,' and 'Follow your nose from front door to three rabbit holes in a row. One of them may prove your goal.'

This took a jolly long time to do, as you can imagine; in fact we spent days over it, all through the bad weather, and for once Cecilia was quite helpful and thought up some ingenious clues.

'You ought to have been jolly well wrecked on a treasure island in the Caribbean in the days of the buccaneers,' I said. 'I bet you'd have got to the treasure first.'

Cecilia pointed out, quite rightly, that it was a lot easier to make up clues than to follow them.

'Don't be too ingenious,' said Mrs York, 'or nobody will find anything and then they'll all be wanting their money back, and what we need is the money.'

Then the weather cleared up and was sunny and mild and not like November at all, so three days before the bazaar we went out and buried the tins with the help of the plan we had made. Each clue was now in a sealed envelope with fifteen pence written on the outside, which was what the competitors had to pay for it, and as the prizes were jolly good it was worth it.

In a way the break from practices had been a good thing, because everybody turned up keen and anxious to make up for the lost time. By now all the ponies had got used to the record player, even when it was on full blast, so we didn't think there was anything to fear from the local band who were going to play on the day. The tunes we had chosen were *Colonel Bogey* and *Blaze Away*, because they are gay and have the right beat and somehow all ponies seem to like them; though Cecilia was rather disdainful and said, 'Gosh, what taste! Some people don't know anything about music. Couldn't you have had *Swan Lake*?'

We hastily pointed out that this wasn't a ballet but a pony-ride, and Cecilia said she was afraid that that was going to be only too obvious.

Ann and I were shaking at the knees by now, because we felt that if the musical ride wasn't a success, although Mrs York would be too kind to criticize, we should go home with our heads in the dust, so to speak. Our professional reputation and the whole prestige of equitation seemed to be at stake.

'I'd feel happier if it wasn't for Rose and Arthur,' I said gloomily. 'I dream about those kids every night, it's a sort of nightmare.'

'I'm more worried about Lucille and John Hicks,' said Ann. 'He hates riding with her and he doesn't bother to help her to keep level. He keeps the pace and length himself and leaves her to muddle along. It's jolly selfish of him.'

'I suppose I'd better have a word with him,' I said. 'I'll put it down in my book under *Things I have Got To Do*, and there are twenty-two of them already.'

'What's the first?' said Ann, and I said it was Grooming and Tack Cleaning On The Day.

As we felt this was terribly important we gave the team a special lecture on it, and it seemed to sink in.

'Nothing but perfection will do,' I said, and Ann said afterwards that I sounded like our late lamented head-mistress at school.

'What are we going to wear?' asked Althea. 'It'll be too cold for white shirts and jodhs.'

'I vote, black coats and hard hats,' said Nan Bruce. 'We might as well look terrifically high-class.'

There was a shriek at this, as it turned out that only about four of the sixteen had got black coats.

'But we can't all wear different jackets,' said Pamela Shooter. 'We shall look so odd.'

'Jackets are dull, anyway,' said Judy. 'Let's all wear our velvet caps and turtle neck jerseys, all different colours.'

'Velvet caps are okay,' said Ann, 'and jerseys sound right, but help! Not all different colours!'

'What colours have you got?' I said.

It turned out that everybody could lay hands on either a yellow or a white jersey, so we suggested that they should bring the jerseys on the day and we would pool them and put each pair of people into the same colour.

'And just see,' I added, 'that everybody's jodhpurs are clean and fit properly.'

I put that bit in because I know from my vast experience that when a show day comes some lazy people have forgotten to get their jodhs cleaned, so they hastily borrow their sister's, which either hang down in swags or are so tight that the wearer looks like a wooden doll.

'Can I wear my new yellow gloves?' asked Janet Watts.

Everybody howled.

'No she can't!' said Nan Bruce. 'We haven't all got new yellow gloves.'

I then rubbed it in about shoes being polished, and no revelation of luminous pink socks or anything like that.

John Hicks said in disgust, 'Crumbs! Is this a riding practice or a mannequin parade?' He said that for two pins he'd take himself and his palomino out of it, and because we wanted the palomino so much because it gave tone to the team, we managed to calm John down.

At last everybody went home, and Ann said after all that arguing she felt like a shadow that had lost its body.

I said that, talking of shadows, it was nice to feel we had a good lunch to go to instead of one of Mrs Sound's meals which weren't there.

After lunch we gave ourselves a treat by going for a long ride on my ponies, across hill and down dale. Cecilia came too, on her bicycle, and criticized our riding most of the way. When we had had enough of this we turned into some woods where she couldn't follow us on her bike, and thus lost her. It sounds a bit mean, but she brought it on herself.

9
The Usefull Charmes

'JUST listen to this,' said Ann.

It was a pouring wet afternoon and we were sitting in the morning-room, Cecilia madly making pincushions out of pink felt, me just as madly darning my only decent pair of tights, and Ann reading a funny old book which she had dug out of a cupboard.

'This is comic,' she went on. 'It's a chapter called *Usefull Charmes* and here's one called "a charme for good weather on the Festal Daye".'

'What festal day?' asked Cecilia who has no imagination.

'Any festal day, you dope,' I said. 'The day you dance round the maypole, or the day the beautiful village maiden gets married, or anything you want a fine day for. Like the bazaar.'

'I don't see why we need a fine day for the bazaar particularly,' said Cecilia maddeningly. 'It's all in the house, anyway.'

'What about our little equestrian show?' I said coldly.

'Well really, Jill, you can't say it's important,'

said Cecilia. 'I mean, the bazaar wouldn't conk out without it.'

'Come off it!' said Ann. 'People will want to look at something decent and exciting when they're sick of gazing at your beastly pincushions. And I think you've got a nerve and a half saying that our show isn't important. Mrs York must think it's important or she wouldn't have bothered to have us staying here all this time.'

'Honk-honk, she's got you there!' I chortled. 'Go on about the charm, Ann. You were saying some-it.'

'It tells you what you have to do,' said Ann. 'You get some horse hairs and tie one tightly round each finger of your left hand. We could manage that. Then you wash your hands carefully in a "brew made of clover picked by ye light of ye moon". Gosh, do you think there's any clover around in November?'

'There's some in the kitchen garden, I saw it,' I said. 'In fact the gardener was just going to root it out, but it'll be on the rubbish heap. How do we brew it?'

'Just in a teapot in the ordinary way,' said Cecilia sarkily.

'No you don't, chum,' said Ann. 'You pour boiling water over it, and let it simmer. Well, okay, we've got our hands washed, and next we have to go into the woods and find a latch tree –'

'A what tree?' I said.

'It says a latch tree.'

'She means a larch tree,' said Cecilia. 'The girl can't read.'

'It says a latch tree,' said Ann, 'and if it says a latch tree it jolly well means a latch tree. This is a sensible book. Don't tell me in all the woods round this house there isn't a latch tree.'

'You've got my permission to go and find one,' said Cecilia. 'I shan't stop you. I couldn't care less.'

'What do you do when you've found the latch tree?' I asked.

'You walk round it three times with your eyes shut, and say, "Sun, Sun, come if you may, shine upon our festal day." That's all.'

'Let's do it,' I said. 'It'll be fun. Let's put our macks on and go and get the horse hairs out of Black Boy's tail, and find the clover and get it brewed while there's nobody in the kitchen.'

'How childish can people get?' said Cecilia.

'That's what I thought when I saw you making those silly pincushions,' I said, and felt very pleased with myself, because it was the first time in my whole life I had thought of the right thing to say at the right moment. One usually thinks of it about twelve hours too late.

Ann and I got the scissors and went down to the farm and cut ten hairs carefully out of Black Boy's long tail, though he looked at us as if he thought we were mad, and I expect we were a bit.

Then we went to the rubbish heap, and sure enough there were heaps of wet green clover. The charm didn't say how much to use, so we got two good handfuls. There was nobody in the kitchen, as Mrs York's maid always had a lie down on her bed between two and three in the afternoon, and so did Mrs York.

We put the clover into a pan and poured boiling water over it, and let it simmer on the gas ring for about five minutes. Then we washed our hands in it. It felt a bit funny and messy, and we were glad when it was done. We poured the water away, threw the boiled clover in the refuse can, and thankfully dried our hands.

'What's the next thing?' I asked.

'Oh murder!' said Ann. 'We ought to have tied the horse hairs round our fingers before we washed our hands! Now we'll have to do it all over again.'

'You absolute clot!' I said. 'Well, you can jolly well get some more clover and boil it. Let's tie the hairs on each other.'

This took ages. I don't know if you've ever tried tying horse hairs round somebody's fingers – I don't suppose you've ever done anything so batty – but having started this we simply had to go on. The horse hairs were stiff and kept coming untied, it was a frightful business. However, at last it was done, and Ann got some more clover and we went through the whole washing and tidying up process again.

'Now we've had it!' I said. 'It's going to be dark before we can get into the woods and find this latch tree.'

At that moment Mrs York came into the kitchen and said, 'What on earth are you girls doing?'

We told her, and added, 'I expect you'll think we're bats.'

She began to laugh, and said, 'I think it's rather fun.'

'We've left it a bit late,' I said, 'because now we've got to go into the woods to find a latch tree and we don't even know what it is.'

'Do you think it means a larch?' said Ann. 'And even if it does, I don't know how we're going to find one.'

'Oh, it's easier than that,' said Mrs York. 'A latch tree is what the local people call a tree in the park that has a fence round it to keep the cattle from rubbing against it. There's one right outside the side door.'

'Why, that's marvellous,' I said. 'Come on, Ann, bring the book and let's get it right.'

Mrs York was so intrigued that she came with us and we all crept out of the house giggling.

'Now shut your eyes,' said Mrs York when we got

to the latch tree, 'and feel your way round it, and I'll tell you when you've gone round three times.'

'Wait,' I said. 'Let's learn this comic poetry off by heart first. If we say it wrong we'll probably bring down a hurricane.'

It wasn't hard to learn, and Ann and I went groping our way round the tree saying, 'Sun, Sun, come if you may, shine upon our festal day.'

By now we were all pretty wet, and Mrs York said that she thought some tea and hot buttered buns would meet the case, so we helped her to make these and took them into the morning-room.

'You don't mean to say you've been doing that silly rubbish?' said Cecilia, looking at our wet hair. 'You want your heads examining.'

'In that case,' said Mrs York, 'I must want mine examining too, because I've been doing the silly rubbish with them.'

You never in your life saw anybody so completely squashed as Cecilia. She couldn't say a word, and then in the end she gulped, and said, 'I do hope the charm works because we do want a fine day on the day.' Which was quite a climb-down for Cecilia.

To make a long story short, the charm worked! On the day of the bazaar we woke up to see the sky a lovely clear pale blue, and soon the sun came up and it shone all day. The grass in the park sparkled, it was going to be just right for the ride and the treasure hunt. Ann and I spent the morning inspecting our 'props', while Mrs York and some of her friends and Cecilia got the stalls ready in the drawing-room and dining-room, and laid the buffet tables for tea in the hall and the morning-room.

Everything went well, and Mrs York laughed and said we had better try a few more charms as we were so good at it. When the preparations were finished, we had sandwiches, coffee, and bananas in the kitchen as it was the only room that wasn't full of bazaar, and then Ann and I went upstairs to get dressed.

We had decided to wear our white turtle-necks, and light jodhpurs, as we thought this would match the team and also look a bit glamorous, but when I opened my drawer to get out the jersey I gave a scream of horror.

The day before I had thrown in my red silk head scarf and it was damp with rain, and the red had run all on to my beautiful white jersey in streaks.

'Gosh!' said Ann. 'That's torn it. Now what are you going to do?'

'I've simply had it,' I wailed. 'Now I've nothing to wear but my old blue one, I shan't match, and I shall look like a tramp and it's all my own fault. I never thought of the red running.'

I was miserable too because I knew I was to blame. Mummy had told me ten million times about throwing things into drawers wet because I couldn't be bothered to hang them on the rack and dry them, and now I was well and truly caught out.

Just then Cecilia passed the open door and heard my shrieks of anguish.

'What on earth's the matter?' she said.

'Jill's ruined her white jersey,' said Ann, holding it up.

'Well, she shouldn't have thrown a wet red thing on it,' said Cecilia.

'Do you think I don't know that,' I yelled. 'I could murder you!'

'I'll tell you what,' said Cecilia. 'I'll lend you mine, as it's all in aid of the bazaar.'

I nearly fell down dead.

'You don't mean your new one?' I said. 'You've only worn it once.'

'It's okay,' said Cecilia. 'You can wear it.'

As this was the most noble thing my cousin had ever done in her life I was completely overcome.

'I say, that's terrific of you,' I said. 'Thanks very much, Cecilia.'

'I'll get it for you,' she said. 'And perhaps you won't be such a careless idiot in future.'

So when Ann and I were ready we really did look magnifique. Then our pony people began to arrive, and all our fears were at rest because they looked magnifique too. One kid's mother had tied a pink scarf round its neck in case it got a sore throat, but we soon had that off. We stood them all in a row and made them give a final rub to their boots and put their caps straight. Then we inspected the ponies, and believe me, they were decently groomed too, except for one or two minor items which we soon put right.

Of course everybody had butterflies, and Janet moaned, 'I know I shan't pivot properly in the fours,' and her partner said, 'If you don't you'll wreck the whole thing'; and Noel said, 'If she wrecks the whole thing I'll absolutely pulverize her,' and Janet said, 'What's pulverize?' and her partner said, 'Something absolutely beastly.'

'For goodness' sake shut up,' I said, 'and don't put everybody else off.'

Crowds of people rolled up for the bazaar which started off with a whack, everybody madly buying things from Mrs York's stall. Ann and I felt we must do something for Cecilia after she'd been so atomically decent about the white jersey, so we went to her stall upon which sat all those revolting-looking tea-cosies and pincushions which weren't selling too well, and I said I would like to buy a tea-cosy for Mummy, and deliberately chose the most hideous one which I knew nobody else would be mad enough to buy, and Ann cottoned on to the idea and bought a pincushion for her mother.

Cecilia beamed and said, 'Thanks frightfully. There's nothing like a thing of beauty, is there?'

I could have said that my idea of a thing of beauty wasn't pea green with yellow squiggles, but I was noble enough not to. After all, I had on the white jersey in all its pure unsullied beauty.

By now the tea provided by Mrs York was going with a swing, like tea at bazaars always does. You wouldn't think people wanted tea at three o'clock in the afternoon, but at bazaars they always do, and I must say the sandwiches and cakes looked out of this world. Looking at them was about all that Ann and I got, because by now the people who were riding in our team had begun to drift around the tearoom, eating cakes, and saying, 'I say, what time do we start?' and we were afraid we should never get them rounded up.

I said to Mrs York, 'Please do you think you could tell everybody that the Musical Ride is just about to take place, or they'll go on eating for ever, and so will our team.'

'Right ho,' said Mrs York, and she clapped her hands, and a hush fell. It sounded funny when everybody stopped rattling cups and jabbering.

'The Musical Ride is about to start,' said Mrs York, 'and I can assure you it's going to be good. Whatever you do, don't miss it. Jill and Ann, here, have been training the boys and girls for ages, and when you see them you'll be just thrilled. So please will everybody go out to the front of the house.'

'I wish she hadn't laid it on so thick,' I murmured

to Ann as we crawled away. 'It makes me feel more wobbly than ever.'

There waiting outside was the local band in red uniforms. When everything was ready and the riders drawn up and the crowd assembled, they started to play *Colonel Bogey*, and we were off.

Oh, how careful everybody was! After a while, when we saw that it was going properly and that nothing awful was going to happen, Ann and I started breathing again after holding our breaths till we nearly burst.

I can't say it was perfect, but the spectators seemed to think it was, especially the mothers of the riders; and after it was over they asked for it to be done again, and a photographer from the local paper took pictures, and Mrs York's helpers picked up a huge collection of money.

Then the fond mothers clustered round Ann and me and said what marvellous teachers we were, and we went very red and murmured, 'Oh, not really!' and modest mutterings like that, and the photographer said, could he have a photo of us two together?

(The pictures appeared next day in the local paper, and Ann looked really glamorous and about nineteen, and I had my eyes shut and my cap had slipped, and I looked about twelve. This is the sort of thing that happens to me.)

The next item was the treasure hunt in which

absolutely everybody in the neighbourhood who could dig up a pony had entered.

Three of the Pobley children who had only one pony between them were in it, sharing the pony, and Dulcie Willow turned up on the most beautiful grey mare you ever saw, and a woman who looked about ninety and had been hunting all her life turned up, all smiles and cracking jokes and riding side-saddle.

Ann and I sold the envelopes with the clues, and the money fairly rolled in. There was some confusion while people read their clues and tried to make out what they meant, then somebody would go streaming away across the park, only to discover a tin with a blank paper in it. Then he or she would come back to pay another fifteen pence for another clue.

The first home to get a prize was Dulcie Willow, and her prize was a pair of glass jam dishes for which I wouldn't have thanked you, but Dulcie thought they were super.

Josephine Pobley won a large iced cake which – believe it or not – she and her two brothers devoured in about five minutes, and the Ancient Huntress, as Ann had christened her, won a lipstick in a case.

Then to our surprise Cecilia appeared, and said, 'You patronized my stall so I'll have a go at your show, a girl has lent me a pony.'

I felt a bit doubtful, as Cecilia on a pony has to be seen to be believed, and is apt to spread death and destruction around, but who was I to argue, so I took her fifteen pence; and the last thing I saw of her, she was mounted on a pony and cantering off into the misty stretches of the park where it was now beginning to go dusk. I never gave her another thought until the girl whose pony she'd borrowed came and said she wanted to go home, and where was her pony?

'Hasn't Cecilia come back?' I said, and the girl said, 'She must be at Southampton by now.'

I thought, if Cecilia was never seen again, her mother, my aunt, would blame me for letting her go off like that, as if anybody could stop Cecilia from doing anything she wanted to do!

Then Mrs York came out and said that Cecilia had rung up. The pony had galloped for about three miles before she could stop him, and a nice woman whose cottage she had nearly bashed into had asked her in and given her a second cup of tea and let her sit by the fire, and had kindly rubbed the pony down. And would somebody come and fetch them?

Mrs York sent off the farmer with the horse-van, and Cecilia and the pony arrived back without a hair out of place.

'Gosh!' I said bitterly. 'What luck you do have. If

it had been me I'd have got into a frightful scrape.'

By now everything at the bazaar had been sold, and Mrs York was dizzy with bliss over the money she had got for the refugees. All the sixteen riders in our team were given boxes of chocolates for their hard work, and went home very thrilled.

'The whole day has been the most terrific success,' said Mrs York, 'and a lot of it has been due to you girls. It certainly was a lucky day for me when I met you, and darling Cecilia too.

'As none of you had a chance to win any prizes for yourselves,' went on Mrs York, 'I am going to give you each one.'

She put a small parcel into each of our hands, and when we opened them we found in each of them a lovely blue enamel bracelet.

We stuttered our thanks, and said, 'We've simply loved being here, and we wish it was all beginning instead of ending.'

This was true, as we had already realized that our job at Pockett House had ended now the bazaar was over, and we couldn't help wondering what was going to happen to us next. What did happen was that we both had letters from our mothers, saying that Christmas was coming and we must both be home in time for it. Of course we wanted to be home for Christmas.

'But we don't want to stay at home for ever,' said

Ann to Mrs York sorrowfully. 'We'd love to have another pony job, but they're not easily come by and we don't know where we'll find one.'

'You'll find one,' said Cecilia, who was also preparing to go home. 'I never saw anybody like you two for falling on your feet.'

'I might even be able to hear of a job for you,' said Mrs York. 'If I do, I'll ring you up after Christmas.'

We said that would be marvellous, and after thanking her again for all the fun we'd had at Pockett House, we set off home for Chatton with a terrific story of adventures to tell.

10
Lucky again

MUMMY said she hoped I was cured of going out into the wide, wide world in search of adventures, and I said on the contrary I was looking forward to more. She roared with laughter over all our mishaps at Little Chimneys Farm, and was excited about the lovely time we had had with Mrs York, and then began to see my point of view.

'Only don't count too much on Mrs York finding you a job,' she said. 'She may not know of anything or she may forget.'

'Whatever it is,' I said, 'I don't suppose it will be as good as it was at her house, but it would be fun to see what turns up.'

But I wished Mummy hadn't said that about Mrs York forgetting, because it struck chill upon my beating heart. (This poetical phrase I got out a of a book, but I really did feel like that.)

I asked Ann, did she think Mrs York would forget? And she said that even if Mrs York did we couldn't do anything about it because we should be making a nuisance of ourselves, and *her* mother would be livid if we did that.

We decided that we wouldn't start worrying until after Christmas and New Year, but on January 2nd we would start worrying. We went into Ryechester to buy Christmas presents for our nearest and dearest, and as usual I wished I was a millionaire as I turned the few sordid coins over in my purse. Talking of purses, I bought Mummy a very nice one made of red leather, and Ann bought her mother a scent spray.

Ann and I decided that for once we wouldn't give each other horsy presents, so I bought her a diary – blue with gold edges – and she bought me a bottle of bath essence called Dew of Lotus, because I couldn't imagine what this scent would be like and I had to try it. It sounded too glamorous for words, but the first time I used it Mummy came rushing upstairs shrieking, 'Is something burning? There's a most ghastly smell all over the house.'

It is funny that dew of lotus should smell of burning socks, but it did.

Well, Christmas was over and we took down the paper chains and the holly, and put away the balloons and the silver fir cones and red ribbons for next year, and put the Christmas cards into a box so that we shouldn't forget anybody next time, and finished the last of the chocolates and the last bit of the Christmas cake, and I wrote all my thank-you letters.

I had had a Christmas card from Mrs York and

so had Ann, so she hadn't forgotten us, but as the days went by we came to the sad conclusion that she wasn't going to do anything about another job for us.

When the first of February came I sensed a change in the home atmosphere. Mummy began muttering darkly that it was time I did something, and I myself felt that it was, because the holidays were over, but Mummy's ideas of 'Something' and mine were so gruesomely different.

The crisis came that very afternoon when Ann arrived and announced that her mother had put her down for a course in Flower Arrangement so that she could Take It Up Seriously, and get a job with a very good florist in Ryechester.

I told her I didn't know she was any good at Flower Arrangement, and she said she wasn't, but her mother thought she ought to be, and she had to go to this place on Monday morning and they would teach her all about chicken wire and pin-holders and things.

'If only Mrs York would phone!' said Ann. 'Even if she didn't know of any job, at least we'd know she hadn't forgotten about us.'

She sounded desperate. I was very blue. It was a hopeless prospect, you must admit, and I could see poor Ann being swept away into the jaws of this Flower-arranging place and me into something equally sordid. Of course we couldn't hang about doing nothing, we realized that, and we wanted to work, but it was sad to see our beautiful dreams coming to naught.

That very afternoon I had just come into the kitchen from feeding the ponies when the telephone rang. Mummy answered it and said calmly, 'It's for you, Jill. It's Mrs York.'

I rushed to the phone, so breathless and excited that I could only stutter.

Mrs York said, 'Is that you, Jill?' and I said, 'Yes, it is,' and my voice came out in a squeak like a day-old chick.

By the time she had finished talking and rung off I was in a pink-coloured trance, but I soon came out of it when Mummy started telling me off for going straight from the stable to the sitting-room without changing my shoes.

About half an hour later I was charging up to Ann's house on my bike. She saw me from the window and rushed out.

'What on earth is it?'

'Shhh!' I said. 'Mrs York has phoned.'

Ann's house is the kind of place where you have to say Shhh! otherwise everybody wants to know why you've come and join in your private conversation.

'Come on up,' said Ann, nearly bursting with excitement and we went up to her room and flopped on the bed.

'It's a job!' I said,

'No kidding?'

'Absolutely not. I can hardly believe it myself. She rang up about half an hour ago. The job is with somebody called Miss Day. She's an old, old friend of Mrs York's, and she has a large farm with lots of room, and knows everything there is to know about pigs and chickens, but nothing about ponies and, –'

'Oh Christmas!' shrieked Ann. 'Don't tell me we've got to go and teach somebody about eighty, who's a friend of Mrs York's, to ride a pony?'

'Will you shut up and listen till I've done?' I said. 'Miss Day has two nieces from Australia staying with her, and she thinks it would be nice for them to learn to ride and also have some young companionship – that's us – so would we like to go, and we'll stay at the farm and she'll pay for the use of my ponies, and pay us a salary too. Can you imagine? Isn't it super?'

'I don't know,' said Ann, biting her nails. 'That young companionship bit gets me. Are these nieces dotty, or something? Why can't they be young companions to each other?'

'Oh, don't you go all cautious and prudent!' I said. 'What's the matter with you? Don't you realize our lives are saved? Or do you *want* to go and stick flowers into chicken wire for the rest of your days? I think you're the depths.'

Ann said she didn't mean to be the depths, but

somehow the job wasn't exactly what she'd visualized. She had pictured something much more glamorous and promising in the world of equitation.

I bounced on the bed and a spring gave way with a loud ping.

'What's the matter with you?' I said. 'Beggars can't be choosers.'

'We haven't begged for anything,' said Ann, 'but as for teaching two little kids to ride – Going all the way back again to the dreary "Mount like this" and "Sit like this", and leading them round on a rein. I thought we'd done with that for ever. If only we could have had a job exercising hunters!'

'Well, we haven't had one offered,' I said crossly. 'And we have had this job offered, and I thought you'd have been running round in circles, yelping hurray. You'd better go and arrange your beastly flowers.'

'Oh, not likely!' said Ann. 'We'll try the job, but you must admit it sounds grue, being stuck on a farm with two kids and some pigs and chickens, and a woman called Miss Day who isn't horsy and knew Mrs York a hundred years ago.'

'If we don't like it,' I said, 'we can always come home.'

'No we can't. They'll laugh at us and say we can't keep a job.'

'Look,' I said, 'are we going or not? Because if we are, don't beef about it,' and she finally said, okay.

Then we went downstairs to tell Mrs Derry, who had been hoping all along that Mrs York wouldn't ring at all. However, the one thing that pleased Mrs Derry was the fact that this job sounded so dull and tame, because she had been afraid that somebody would offer us a job in a circus, so she said that Ann could go if she liked, but she'd soon be bored stiff and glad to come home.

So a week later we landed at Mayside Farm, complete with our luggage and Black Boy and Rapide. It was a pretty farm and very well kept, and the house itself was all chintzy, and the weather was springlike and pussy-willowish, and Miss Day was the fussy kind. She seemed to spend her whole life dreaming about pigs and chickens, and she looked at my ponies as if she expected them to grunt or peck.

'I don't know the first thing about them,' she said. 'But I've got a nice stable that has never been used, and I've told the corn shop that you're to order just what you need for them.'

This sounded promising, and actually the arrangements for the ponies were even better than I could have wished. We were then shown what looked like thousands of white chickens and pink pigs and we said we thought they looked jolly nice, and Miss Day beamed. She was very small and had on an enormous pair of dungarees, and her hair was in little screwed-up curls.

Then she took us in the house and gave us each a glass of milk, and opened a huge tin of chocolate biscuits, and said, 'I know what little girls like'; which was the right idea, though we weren't very sold on being called little girls when we were sixteen, and we would rather have had tea than milk but didn't like to say so.

'The children are out somewhere,' she said. 'They love playing in the woods, I expect it's being Australian, all those wide open spaces, you know.'

Ann looked at me and made a face, and I glared at her.

'You see my idea, don't you?' said Miss Day. 'Go on, have some more chocolate biscuits. All the children about here seem to ride, and I thought it would be nice if my nieces could learn too, it would give them something to do, so I asked them if they'd like to, and they said they didn't mind trying.'

My spirits sank a lot. The 'children' began to sound pretty grim to me, what with playing in the woods and saying they didn't mind trying to learn to ride. I daren't look at Ann.

We then went up to our room, a very nice one, and sat down on our beds, and Ann said, 'We've had it! Milk, and pink pigs, and two little woodsy kids from the wide open spaces who've never ridden on a pony and think they'd like to try. My Russian rabbits!'

'Oh shut up!' I said, which wasn't clever, but I just felt bad. 'You go home if you want to,' I went on. 'Probably with a most terrific effort I might even teach these kids all by myself. I seem to remember having done similar things in my youth.' I thought this last bit sounded frightfully grand and sarky.

'Oh, I'll stick it out,' said Ann. 'We'll review the position after a week. By then we'll know if they're possible or hopeless. But I won't read fairy tales to them, or nurse their teddies.'

'Girls! Girls!' came from below.

'There she goes,' I said. 'We'd better go down.'

The 'children' had come home. From the way that Miss Day had treated us, as though we were six, I suppose we ought to have realized. Our new riding pupils were twins, and about our own age, in fact a bit taller than either of us.

11
Two duds

'THIS is Norrie,' said Miss Day, 'and this is Dorrie. And this is Jill, and this is Ann.'

'Hullo,' we said.

'Hullo,' said the twins without enthusiasm. They looked a bit glum.

'Now you four get to know each other,' said Miss Day, 'and I'll buzz off.'

When she had gone I said, 'We've got to teach you two to ride.'

'That's the idea,' said one of them, I don't know which.

'Do you want to?' said Ann.

'We don't mind,' said the other one. 'It'll please Auntie and it won't hurt us.'

'It might hurt us,' I said. 'I like teaching people who really want to learn.'

'That's all right,' said one of them. 'We'll have a go. I don't suppose you want to start now. We don't. Let's give it a miss till tomorrow, we've been out all afternoon and we've had enough fresh air to last us for ages.'

'I thought you came from the wide open spaces,' said Ann, 'where you never get anything else but fresh air?'

'Actually,' said the other one, 'we come from Sydney, but that wouldn't mean a thing to Auntie. She thinks Australia's one big dustbowl full of sheep.'

I began to giggle, and one of the twins said, 'What's on your mind?'

'We thought you were little kids,' I said. 'We thought you played in the woods and we'd have to read fairy tales to you.'

Later on, Ann said to me, 'I don't see this job lasting long. These people are practically grown up, like us. They'll learn to ride well enough to satisfy Miss Day in about two weeks. Then she'll have to hire or buy ponies for them, and we shall go home.'

But it didn't turn out like that. I have met some duds in my time. In my long and chequered career I have taught people who didn't know which way round a saddle went on, and were absolutely incapable of understanding simple orders like Hands Down and Knees Up, and did the wrong thing instinctively, but never, never have I encountered such supercharged clots as Norrie and Dorrie when you tried to put them on a pony.

I led out Black Boy as he was used to beginners, and had the sweetest nature and really tried to help people, and was so patient.

'Now come on, Norrie,' I said. 'I'll help you up so that you can get the feel of sitting in the saddle.'

I helped her up, and she promptly fell off the other side. I did it again, and she did it again.

'How *do* you keep on, anyway?' she said helplessly.

'Have you ever heard of balance?' I said sarkily. 'Have you ever sat on a chair? Well, just *sit*!'

Norrie said she'd have another try, and this time she clung on as if she was sitting on the top of a peak with a hundred-foot drop on all sides. Then she said she was giddy and could she get off!

By then I was worn out, so I told Ann to have a go with Dorrie. It took ages to get Dorrie up, and when she was up somehow she was facing backwards. It sounds incredible, but she was and had to begin all over again. The second time she got her arms round Black Boy's neck.

'Let go and sit *up*!' yelled Ann.

'I daren't,' shrieked Dorrie.

Ann mopped her brow and said, 'This is killing me.'

I agreed. In all our wide experience, with all the kids we had taught, we had never never come across such duds. It took us one hour to get Norrie and Dorrie even to sit in the saddle like pokers.

Norrie said, 'If ever the pony moved I should die.'

I said, 'You two are the depths,' and Dorrie said

they thought we were too tough with them, which struck us dumb.

When we went in for lunch Miss Day said, 'Well, how did the pupils get on?' Ann and I said nothing, and Dorrie murmured that it was harder than they'd thought, and Miss Day said, 'Really? Quite little children seem to do it so easily,' which didn't add to the gaiety.

We lammed into the food.

I know I say a lot about food in my books, and Mummy puts a pencil through about half of what I have written, but I think it is interesting.

I don't know if you have ever stayed on a pig and poultry farm like Miss Day's, but it is logical to suppose that one would get nothing to eat but chicken and pork. We had chicken and pork in every shape and form, and mostly the lopsided bits that didn't go down well with the buyers. At first Ann and I adored it, but to make a long story short, by the time we left Mayside Farm we never wanted to eat those two things again as long as we lived.

However, apart from never seeing any other animal on the table, as though they didn't exist, the meals were always very good, and Miss Day had the right idea about puddings, which were spongy, jammy, and supersonic.

After lunch we expected there would be another pony lesson, but Norrie and Dorrie just announced that they were going out, and proceeded to disappear. On bikes.

'Do you see that?' I said to Ann. 'Bikes. And they can't sit on a pony.'

'I expect they're made wrong,' she said. 'Gosh, I do like those tapered black slacks they've got, and those super mohair sweaters.'

'Never mind their sweaters,' I said morosely. 'They'll be the death of me. After I'd had Dorrie on a leading rein for five minutes, shrieking her head off, I tell you I could have gone into orbit.'

Ann said she would rather teach two-year-old babies any day, and it struck me we had quite a job on our hands. At this rate we would be at Mayside Farm for years. I suppose there are some people who are incapable of learning to ride, but I didn't think that I should ever come up against any! I even began to wonder how soon it would be fair to tell Miss Day that she was wasting her time and money, and that her beauteous dream of seeing her dear nieces on steeds of fiery disposition was all washed up.

However, the girls had gone out and Ann and I didn't seem to have anything to do, so we asked Miss Day if it would be all right for us to go for a ride, and she said, 'Do, dears, do.' So we did. We had a wonderful ride on my ponies, and found some heath land to gallop over, and thoroughly enjoyed ourselves. The country around was marvellous, and

Ann said, 'Well, even if we do work ourselves to death in the mornings and nearly break our horsy hearts, it's worth it for rides like this.'

Norrie and Dorrie came back about six, without saying where they'd been. After supper I felt I ought to do a bit for my living, so told them that we'd have a session on The Care of the Horse, round the dining-room table. They didn't seem very keen, but I did my best, and if they didn't take it in that wasn't my fault. We ended up by playing Scrabble.

Next morning I felt in the mood of a slave driver, so I led them to the stable and made them muck out, groom the ponies, mix the feeds, give water, etc., etc., all under my eagle eye and supervision. They were very ham-handed and took ages. I said sarkily, 'Well, well! We'll just about be done in time for lunch. How on earth would you manage if you wanted to be out early or go hunting?'

Norrie said that she couldn't imagine them ever wanting to be out early, and they were never likely to go hunting, and Ann said, 'You're telling me!'

Eventually we got them out into the paddock, and led them round on leading reins. Imagine, at their age! As soon as we left them alone they slid round the ponies' necks or got their feet tangled in the stirrup leathers.

At lunch Miss Day again asked for a progress report, and Dorrie said, 'I think we're getting on.'

It was more than Ann and I thought, but we let it pass.

In the afternoon we tried again. How we worked! The ponies must have been as fed up as we were, but by tea time Norrie and Dorrie could actually ride a slow and wobbly circle, all by themselves.

'I've got hopes,' I said to Ann. 'I should think about another two years and they'll be able to enter for the under-tens showing class. I suppose we can't expect much from the poor little things. They're only sixteen.'

We laughed it off. The only thing you could do with Norrie and Dorrie was to see the funny side. I wanted to show them how to rub down the ponies, feed them, and put them up for the night, but Ann said if I did we'd still be in the stable at midnight, so we did it ourselves.

In the evening I got out the horse-book and showed them pictures of the various kinds of tack and taught them the names, or tried to, and told them what everything was for.

'Are you trying to work us to death?' said Dorrie. 'I just can't *hold* any more.'

'You haven't held anything yet,' said Ann brutally. 'Tomorrow we're going to teach you to mount properly, and you've got to know the various parts of the tack we're referring to.'

Norrie said they'd rather learn as it came, and as

both Ann and I by then felt like bits of chewed string we gave up for the rest of the evening.

The next day, the girls' idea of 'learning as it came' may have been amusing to the onlooker, but I assure you it wasn't to us. When I said, 'Take the reins in your left hand' they promptly took them in the right. When I said, 'Take hold of the saddle with your right hand,' they grabbed the crownpiece of the bridle. When I said, 'Put your left foot into the stirrup,' they put the tips of their toes in, and I said, 'Right in for, goodness' sake.' And Norrie somehow got her foot upside down and sat down on the ground with a thump.

'Give me strength!' said Ann.

Dorrie said, 'Well, everybody's got to learn, haven't they? Even you had to learn.'

'What you're learning now,' said Ann, 'I learned in five minutes when I was three. Norrie! For goodness' sake, *spring* into the saddle, you're not climbing the Alps, and sit down – don't bounce– oh, my gosh!' Ann shut her eyes as Norrie thudded into the saddle and grabbed the reins for dear life. 'Honestly,' she went on, 'It isn't fair on the ponies. I know Black Boy's angelic, but it's too much to ask.'

Well, in the end Norrie and Dorrie learned to mount a pony. This doesn't sound much – but oh boy! It took about a week. And we never did teach them to dismount properly, off they would slither, so we gave up.

We sat them straight in the saddle, nicely forward, and then shoved their heels down, their knees up and in, and their hands down.

'Now that's all right,' I said. 'Off you go, and stay like you are now.'

Off they went. Gosh! In three minutes their hands were under their chins and their knees sticking out a mile. They looked like two taxis with the doors open. Then Miss Day came out.

'Oh,' she said, 'they can ride! Isn't that splendid! You *have* done well!' Ann and I didn't know whether to laugh or scream, but we decided that the only way to cope was to laugh.

'It's no good taking these two seriously,' I said to Ann, 'or we'll break our hearts. Miss Day is satisfied, and we're having fun here, so let's make the best of it while it lasts.'

Yes, we were having fun at Mayside Farm. Hopeless as Norrie and Dorrie were when they came in contact with ponies, they were very good company. When the morning lesson was over they used to say, 'Thank goodness, we've had our daily dose now, so let's go out and really enjoy ourselves.'

We felt guilty about this, as it didn't seem to be giving Miss Day good value, but all she said was, 'Yes, run along and enjoy yourselves, girls.' So we took her at her word.

We used to go on the bus to the nearest town

where there was an ice rink, and then it was the twins' turn to laugh at Ann and me. They were both wonderful skaters – which again stunned us, as they seemed to have mastered the art of balance on everything but a pony – and they were awfully decent about teaching us and hauling us round until we could go under our own steam. Soon we were enjoying it tremendously. After an hour at the rink we would have ice-cream and then go to the pictures, and come back for supper.

Norrie and Dorrie were both very good at indoor games and taught us some new and riotous ones to play in the evenings, and they also had lots of imagination and made up smashing stories which they used to write out, and read us one instalment every night to keep us guessing.

Ann said, 'Well, honestly, you can't call this a *job*. We're having much too good a time. I think we ought to ask Miss Day if we can help on the farm.'

So we did, but she only said, 'No, no, no! You're here to be company for the girls, that's all I ask, and I'm quite satisfied.'

It was funny really, because when we wrote home we never knew what to say, as we didn't want to give our parents the impression that we were simply playing about, as we should have been promptly dragged home to do something more serious. As it was, every time Mummy wrote she would say, 'Haven't you taught those two girls to ride yet? You seem to be taking a very long time over it.'

I then wrote and pointed out that we really did a lot of chores, and so we did, as the four of us managed the cooking and so forth between us without any great effort, and actually that rather pleased Mummy as she is great nuts on girls being domesticated, and Ann added, 'P.S. Jill makes the most super cakes.' I certainly did make cakes, though I don't know about them being super, but Mummy was appeased.

12
Mysterious

WE had a Mystery on our hands. Three afternoons a week Norrie and Dorrie disappeared. I don't mean they melted into thin air before our very eyes or anything like that. They just said nothing, got on to their bikes, and went off and didn't come back until nearly supper time.

'It's jolly odd,' I said to Ann. 'Where on earth do they go to?'

'Search me!' she said. 'You'd think they'd say.'

But, they never did.

Once I said to them in a casual, nonchalant way, 'Where are you off to?' and Norrie just said, 'Out,' and sprang on her bicycle.

'I suppose it's just that they don't want us around all the time,' said Ann.

'But you'd think they'd say!'

'P'raps they want to go to the rink on their own.'

'But they ride off in the other direction.'

'P'raps that's to put us off.'

'Oh blow Norrie and Dorrie,' said Ann. 'At least

it gives us a chance to have three jolly good rides a week on the ponies, which we couldn't have if they were sticking around all the time.'

This was true, and Ann and I were enjoying our rides very much. It was glorious riding country all around, even better than at home, and we explored every inch of it, galloping the ponies over great open stretches of common and weaving our way through woodland glades.

'You don't know what you're missing,' we said to Norrie and Dorrie as we washed up the supper things. 'If you'd only pull your socks up and learn to ride properly Miss Day would hire you two ponies – she said so – and you'd love it.'

'We've been here a month already,' said Ann, 'and in spite of our positively gruesome efforts on your behalf, all you two can do is amble round the paddock. It's time you were out on the road, but we daren't take you. You'd fall off if you saw a motor bike!'

'Well, we can't help that,' said Dorrie. 'Riding isn't everything.'

'We think it is,' I said. 'And we're supposed to be here to make you think it is. We've got a hope!'

'If we don't want to go out on the road, we don't want to go out on the road and we're jolly well not going to,' said Norrie. 'So that's that.'

We pointed out that Miss Day would be disappointed, but actually she didn't seem to bother.

Then one evening she said she had seen a film of some girls jumping in a gymkhana, and she would love to see Norrie and Dorrie doing that, and did I think they'd be able to by the time the summer Shows came along? Did I? I ask you!

I had to say truthfully that at their present rate of progress they wouldn't be jumping in competitions much before they were fifty, and she said, what a pity.

I said to Norrie, 'You two jolly well ought to learn to jump, it's awful not to be able to.'

'Okay,' she said. 'We'll have a try.'

I would like to draw a veil over the twins' first jumping lesson. We only put a pole on two bricks in the paddock, the sort of thing you'd do if you were teaching the under-sevens, but from the way those two went on you'd think we were asking them to jump Becher's Brook at Aintree.

At last we persuaded Norrie, who was the more daring of the two, to try. Black Boy gave me a look as if to say, 'Blimey! Am I reduced to this?' He then carried Norrie over the pole without the slightest jerk.

She finished up with her hands tangled in his mane, looked back, and said, 'Did I really jump it?'

'No, you didn't,' said Ann. 'Black Boy did it entirely unaided by you. Gosh, that's the sort of jump we give to three-year-old kids.'

'I'll have a go now,' said Dorrie.

She was up on Rapide, and I wickedly didn't change her over to Black Boy. I knew Rapide's little tricks, and I thought it was time Dorrie had a real lesson. I gave her a few brief, elementary jumping instructions and let her go.

Rapide has always been incapable of jumping less than four feet. He's a bit dim in the head that way. Even a pole three inches off the ground is a four-foot jump to him, and so he made it this time. Up he went in his best show ground manner, flicked his heels, and pretended he was doing a triple bar.

I shut my eyes, expecting to find Dorrie's corpse thudding at my feet.

'Okay,' said Ann dryly. 'She's still on.'

Yes, Dorrie was still on. She had her mouth wide open and looked stunned.

'Did I jump?' she said. 'I thought I was in a helicopter.'

'You jumped,' said Ann. 'You jumped about four foot six. I could see four counties between your legs, which isn't done in the best riding circles, and you looked like a sack of oats being chucked over a wall, but you jumped. Now do it again, and try and stay in the saddle this time.'

'Don't, Dorrie, don't,' shrieked Norrie. 'It was awful. That pony's crackers. He thought he was jumping a wall that wasn't there.'

'That's only Rapide's little way,' I said. 'He's all right.'

But Dorrie said she'd had enough.

'Well, try on Black Boy,' I said. 'He'll step over the pole you won't feel a thing.'

'No thanks,' said Dorrie. 'Let's go and have our elevenses. I want to forget it.'

'Oh, you two are feeble!' I said. 'Another week of teaching you and I'll nearly go into orbit.'

This made them a bit huffy, and after we had washed up the lunch things they went out without a word, mounted their bikes, and set off.

'There they go,' I said. 'I wish I knew what they were up to.'

'Well, let's pretend we're great detectives and follow them,' suggested Ann.

'Don't be silly,' I said. 'We've nothing to follow them on but the ponies, and we should look like sleuths, shouldn't we, clattering along behind them and pretending we weren't there.'

'I expect they just go for a bike ride,' said Ann, 'like we go for a pony ride.'

'Well, why don't they ask us to go with them?'

'I suppose because we haven't got bikes.'

'We could hire bikes.'

'Oh, stop nattering,' said Ann. 'I couldn't care less where they go.' But it still remained a mystery, and mysteries always irritate you until you know what they're all about.

'How did the jumping go on?' asked Miss Day at supper.

'I jumped four foot six,' said Dorrie calmly. Ann and I began to giggle.

'Is that good?' asked Miss Day, turning to me.

'Oh, frightfully good,' I said sarkily. 'They'll be riding at Richmond and Hickstead in no time, at this rate.'

Miss Day looked bewildered.

'Richmond is a very nice place, dear,' she said, 'I have some cousins living there, only I don't see why the girls should want to ride there, and I never heard of Hickstead.'

Ann and I tried not to shriek.

Strangely enough, from then on Norrie and Dorrie did begin to make an effort, and improved quite a lot.

'I don't think they tried before,' Anne said to me, 'but now they're getting interested, and they both sit quite decently and don't fool about any more.'

This was true. We even got them on the road, and on the Common, and when we asked Miss Day she hired two ponies from a local stable and the four of us had a ride in the woods and came home feeling pleased with ourselves.

'You're doing us credit at last,' I said to Norrie and Dorrie. 'We've got our professional reputations to think about, and it was getting us down, thinking that we couldn't do anything with you. It would have been awful to go home feeling that we'd failed.'

'Oh, we're sorry,' they said. 'We never looked at it that way. We'll try harder.'

They did try. We got them doing easy jumps and they sat well and looked very nice. We put up four two-foot-six jumps in the paddock – if you have read my other books you will remember that I can make jumps of practically anything – and the girls learned to do this little round in a way that I had to admit was quite passable.

Then to my horror they began to get big-headed about their riding. This was awful.

At lunch one day Norrie said to Miss Day, 'We're getting jolly good at riding *and* jumping. I should think we could enter almost any competition.'

'What!' I yelled.

'Well, so we could. We were absolutely faultless this morning over the jumps, both of us were.'

'My spotty sputnik!' I said. 'Faultless over two-foot-six jumps, and you're sixteen years old. Two-foot-six jumps are what you get in the juniors. You're just beginners.'

'Rot,' said Dorrie. 'Once you've mastered the principles of jumping the height of the jump doesn't matter, you told me that yourself.'

'Are you suggesting,' said Ann, 'that you've mastered the principles of jumping? Don't make me laugh.'

'You're just discouraging,' said Norrie. 'We're better than you think, in fact we're jolly good.'

'All right,' I said. 'You go on thinking so. Perhaps in the summer after we're gone you'll be able to enter for a competition, and then you'll learn. It's the only way.'

'Well, push the jumps up this afternoon,' said Norrie, 'and we'll have a go.'

So we went out and put the four jumps up to four foot. Norrie had Black Boy and Dorrie had Rapide and they both managed to get over the jumps; then they changed ponies and did it again.

'There you are!' said Dorrie. 'We can jump anything.'

'Give me strength!' said Ann. 'Don't you realize that Jill's ponies are trained to show jumping, and they've been doing it for years? It was the ponies who jumped, you just stuck on. You didn't do a thing.'

'Yes we did,' said Norrie indignantly. 'We gave them the aids like you taught us.'

'They'd recognize those aids if they were jumping in their sleep,' said Ann. 'I'd like to see you try on strange ponies.'

'As a matter of fact,' I said to Ann when we were alone, 'they've both developed a bit of style lately. Have you noticed?'

'Absolutely,' said Ann. 'And Norrie's timing surprised me this morning. P'raps they've got hidden talent which our noble efforts are at last bringing into bud. But we mustn't let them think we think so, they're impossible when they're big-headed, and they've nothing to be big-headed about. P'raps after we've gone they'll enter for a few competitions in the summer. That'll larn 'em!'

By now Norrie and Dorrie were being more co-operative in their lessons, and doing exactly what we told them, but I couldn't say they were taking any great interest, and they always seemed glad when the morning lesson was over, which wasn't very flattering to Ann and me.

I'd say, 'Well, I think we'd better knock off now,' and one of them would say, 'thank goodness,' and it annoyed me very much.

'Anybody would think it was an arithmetic class,' I said to Ann. 'Fancy being glad when a riding lesson was over! Gosh, when I was at the stage they're at I used to nearly weep when the lesson was over, I wanted it to go on for ever.'

'It's just that they're not keen,' said Ann, 'and it's no good pretending they are. Miss Day's wasting her money, though I must say, she doesn't seem to mind.'

There was now no question of an afternoon lesson at all. Norrie and Dorrie took it for granted that by lunch time they had done their duty to the ponies, and in the afternoons we either went off together to the ice-rink or to town, or they did their famous disappearing act.

One thing I will say for them, they were very good about mucking out, feeding the ponies, and cleaning tack.

'As a matter of fact,' I said to Ann, 'they seem to like that better than riding, aren't they bats?'

We both decided that Norrie and Dorrie were mild cases of lunacy and left it at that.

It was now the end of March, lovely spring weather and gorgeous for riding. Ann and I came home about five after a wonderful ride, rubbed the ponies down, and sat on the old mounting block in the yard, drinking lemonade. It was one of those afternoons when the girls had vanished, but we had given up bothering about that particular mystery as we didn't seem to have any opportunity for being detectives.

'How long do you think we ought to stop on here?' said Ann. 'I had a letter from Mummy this morning and she's getting restive. Says I've been away two months, and it's time I came home and did some serious thinking. Gosh! As if I didn't do some serious thinking every day of my life.'

'I know,' I said. It's jolly nice here – in a way, we're having a smashing time – but it's a bit of a dead end. We're not getting anywhere ourselves, and we're not learning anything. And between you and me, I don't think Norrie and Dorrie are going to get any further than they are now, not in a million years. P'raps we'd better tell Miss Day we're leaving. We don't want to miss our summer riding in Chatton.'

We decided that we would take the first opportunity to suggest leaving and see how Miss Day took it. Perhaps she was just waiting for us to go but didn't like to say so.

But life still had a shock in store for us.

13
Shock after shock

NORRIE and Dorrie came in that particular evening looking pleased with themselves, and when we sat down to supper Dorrie said, 'What's a point-to-point?'

'It's a race meeting for amateurs,' I said. 'Usually over hurdles, and it's usually got up by the local hunt at the end of the hunting season.'

'Can anybody go in for it?' asked Norrie.

'If they're good enough,' I said. 'But the standard's very high.'

'There's going to be one here on Friday week,' said Dorrie. 'As a matter of fact, we've entered. We thought it would be fun.'

I have been stunned, knocked for six, and pole-axed in my time, but this was the lot. I looked at Ann and she looked at me, and our mouths dropped open, and we sort of yammered at each other.

'That sounds nice, dear, why don't you all enter?' said Miss Day.

'To begin with,' I said, finding my voice, 'Ann and I don't consider ourselves good enough to ride against the local best riders, and as for Norrie and Dorrie – well, I can't imagine what they're think-ing of!'

'Oh, don't be stuffy!' said Norrie.

'If you think,' I said, 'that you're going to ride on my Black Boy and Rapide in the local point-to-point, I can tell you now you've had it. It's fan-tastic. They're not racing ponies. They've never raced in their lives, and they're not going to start now with you two up!'

'Not to worry,' said Dorrie, calmly eating saus-ages. 'We're being lent two horses by a friend.'

'She wants her head examining,' said Ann. 'Has she ever seen you *ride*?'

'Now and then,' said Dorrie.

'Look, Miss Day,' said Ann desperately, 'we don't want to look like spoil-sports and I expect you'll think it isn't our business, but you oughtn't to let the girls do this. It's absolutely beyond them, honestly.'

Miss Day looked bewildered and said, 'Well, I'm no judge, am I, dear? But if they think they can, I don't see why they shouldn't try. After all, we never know what we can do till we try, do we? Or so my mother used to say to me.'

'This is hopeless,' I said, gritting my teeth. I went on, 'As a matter of fact, Miss Day, Ann and I were thinking that it's about time we went home. We've taught the girls all we can and we can't do any more, and we think we ought to get on with some other job now.'

'Well, that's just as you wish, dear,' said Miss Day, smiling amiably. 'But I think you must really stay for another week or so and watch them ride in this point-to-point. It sounds so interesting. Then you could go home on the Saturday.'

'The Saturday!' moaned Ann as we went upstairs later. 'So we're to stay and watch Norrie and Dorrie make fools of themselves and perhaps break their necks, and at the best foul all the other horses, and everybody will say that *we* taught them to ride! This is the end.'

'It may not be so ghastly,' I said. 'After all, there'll only be one under-eighteen event, and they'll probably just trail along at the back and come in last, and if somebody is idiot enough to lend them ponies that's their business. Let's write to our Mums and say we're coming home. That'll be something to look forward to.'

From then on we might just as well have been at home for all we saw of Norrie and Dorrie. They were always going off to their 'friend's' to practice for the point-to-point.

'Say, who is this friend?' murmured Ann. 'Why haven't we heard of her before? And is she the one they've been popping off to in the afternoons?'

'Search me,' I said. 'It's the most fantastic thing. This is the silliest job we ever had, Ann, and I wish we'd never come – only don't let's breathe that at home.'

'At least we've learned to skate,' said Ann.

The next afternoon we thought we'd go for a ride and forget everything. We went a new way, and found ourselves passing some enclosed parkland, and on the edge of the park alongside the road was an enormous notice-board with a huge poster stuck on it.

POINT-TO-POINT MEETING

IN THE PARK

ON FRIDAY MARCH 25TH

FIRST RACE AT 2 P.M.

ENTRIES INCLUDE BEST-KNOWN

COUNTY RIDERS

REFRESHMENTS.

And then something else caught our eye. In red letters.

SPECIAL ATTRACTION

EXHIBITION OF PAIR JUMPING AND

RACING

BY THE FAMOUS CANNON TWINS

(NOREEN AND DOREEN CANNON)

AUSTRALIA'S GIRL RIDING CHAMPION˙

NOW ON HOLIDAY IN THIS COUNTRY

To say that Ann and I were by now staring at each other is an understatement. Our eyes were practically sticking out and meeting. We had often read about the Cannon twins, and how they were supposed to be coming to England in the summer for the big Shows.

Cannon! Noreen and Doreen Cannon! Our brains were clicking like mad and we just couldn't believe it, but it was all falling into place.

We were remembering that we had never once

heard Norrie's or Dorrie's surname. Nobody had ever mentioned it. If we had thought of it at all, we had taken it for granted that it was Day, like their aunt.

'It can't be!' gasped Ann. 'It must be! Are we going mad? And what on earth does it all mean? How did we come into it?'

'Come on,' I said grimly. 'Let's go home and find out.'

Norrie and Dorrie were cheerfully mixing food for the chickens when we got in. Norrie was sitting on the kitchen table singing Waltzing Matilda, while Dorrie doled out the meal into the bucket which Norrie held.

'Hullo, you two,' sang out Dorrie. 'Coming to watch us workers?'

'Oh yes?' I said. 'Would you by any chance ever have heard of the Cannon twins?'

Neither of them turned a hair, and Norrie said, 'I suppose you had to find out some time. But it was fun while it lasted.'

'But what's it all in aid of?' Ann burst out. 'What on earth have you been playing at? And why on earth all these so-called lessons? It's fantastic, it's absolutely bats, isn't it, Jill?'

'Somebody's bats,' I said. 'I've got to the stage when I don't know who.'

'It's quite a story, really,' said Dorrie, giggling. 'I'd better spill the entire thing. It didn't start as a racket, it just grew and grew, didn't it, Norrie?'

'We got so far in, we couldn't get out,' said Norrie. 'Go on, you tell them, Dorrie.'

'Well, it was this way,' said Dorrie. 'Aunt Maud isn't actually our aunt, she's our mother's cousin, and ever since we were born she's been on at Mother to let us come over and stay with her.'

'Over from Australia?' I said.

'That's right. Well, we'd never been to England and we were due here this summer for the Shows, so Mother suggested that we should come over for Christmas and stay with Aunt Maud here until it was time for us to go down south. We'd just got through a heavy two years' riding at home, and with the prospect of an exciting and quite strenuous summer, we all thought a quiet holiday here in the country would be rather good.'

'Quiet is the right word,' said Norrie. 'We'd had a hectic time, and we did need a rest.'

'I bet you did,' said Ann. 'Jill and I have read all about you for ages, and we still can't believe you're actually the Cannon twins.'

'I'm afraid we really are,' said Dorrie. 'Well, let's go on with this gruesome tale. We arrived here at Mayside Farm full of peace and good intentions, only to find that Aunt Maud didn't know who we were, because she didn't know the horsy world existed, if you get me.'

'You mean to say, she didn't know you were the famous Cannon twins?' I yelped.

'Just that,' said Norrie. 'To her we were just her dear little nieces from Australia, and she wanted to find something to amuse us, so one day she saw a jumping competition on a film, and she got the bright idea it would be nice for us to ride like other kids. She suggested this, and just for the joke of it we let her have her way.'

'She was so thrilled at her bright idea,' said Dorrie, 'that we hadn't the heart to spoil it for her. And another thing, we didn't want her to know that we were experienced riders already, because if it once got round the neighbourhood who we were, we'd have been bothered to death by people wanting us to ride for them, and do this and that for them – you can imagine it – and we shouldn't have got any rest from competitive riding at all, and that was what Mother wanted us to have, so that we shouldn't be stale when the British season started. Of course we didn't know what Aunt Maud's ideas would lead to; when we did know we got quite a shock.'

'One day,' said Norrie, taking up the story, 'Aunt Maud came in with a face like the rising moon and told us that she'd heard of two girls who wanted a pony job – preferably to teach riding – and she was going to invite them to come and stay here and TEACH US!'

'We nearly fell flat on our backs,' said Dorrie, 'but we didn't like to say we didn't want you, so we thought we'd wait and see what happened. Then you arrived and we liked you and thought it would be fun to have you here. We talked it over in bed, and decided that we'd play the game Aunt Maud's way and let you jolly well teach us, and we'd be as slow and clottish as we could.'

'Gosh!' said Ann. 'If we'd known what you were really up to we'd have murdered you.'

They rocked with laughing.

'Oh, it was a scream, pretending to be so thick-headed,' shrieked Dorrie. 'And you two were so marvellous. At night, when we got to bed, we used to have the most ghastly pangs of remorse for the trick we were playing on you, but then we were in it up to our necks, and we couldn't give the game away.'

'I don't know how you kept it up,' I said. 'I mean, doing all the wrong things.'

'It was frightfully hard,' said Norrie. 'Once I automatically reined back, and then remembered that you hadn't "taught" me to do that! Fortunately you hadn't noticed me!'

'By that time,' said Dorrie, 'of course we *couldn't* give ourselves away. The explanations would have been too ghastly.'

'I'll say they would,' I said helplessly. 'But now perhaps you'll solve a mystery for Ann and me. *Where did you go in the afternoons?*'

They looked at one another and grinned.

'We went,' said Dorrie simply, 'to a friend of ours a few miles away who keeps a hunting stable. We met him when he was riding in Australia. He let us exercise his horses and get the practice we wanted to keep us in form, and of course he kept our secret.'

'And he persuaded us,' said Norrie, 'to give a show at the local point-to-point. He felt we owed it to the neighbourhood before we went south.'

'Well, that's terrific!' said Ann and I together.

Suddenly I saw Miss Day coming across the yard to fetch the chicken food.

'What are you going to do about *her*?' I asked. 'Tell her?'

'Oh, we couldn't – we couldn't possibly,' gasped Dorrie. 'She'd be furious to think we'd played such a trick on her.'

'I don't think she'd be furious, so much as miserable,' said Norrie, looking blue. 'I begin to feel so low I could crawl under a blade of grass.'

'Never mind,' I said. 'Let's just wait and see what happens at the point-to-point. She'll probably be so thrilled at your riding that she'll forgive you anything.'

14
The point-to-point

WHAT happened at the point-to-point was that Miss Day was so thrilled with the girls' riding that she never even asked any questions, and had nothing to forgive. Instead – but I must tell you what happened.

You should have seen the girls, immaculate in white cord breeches, shining boots, black coats, snowy stocks! In contrast, and not to make ourselves conspicuous seeing we weren't taking any part in the proceedings, Ann and I wore skirts and windcheaters.

'Now I wonder what Miss Day is going to say about these rig-outs?' I said to Ann.

Miss Day didn't see anything extraordinary. She simply looked at the dazzling twins and remarked, 'Very nice, my dears. I suppose that's what people wear for riding. What a pity Ann and Jill aren't riding too, and wearing such nice clothes.'

We nearly went into hysterics.

The car came round and we all set off for the park. There were crowds of people there, and the first thing we did was to go and have a look at the course, which was a snorter as the ground was heavy and some of the hedges high enough to be tricky. All the same, Ann and I would have rather liked to have a try at it, but we hadn't had the practice. Dorrie and Norrie were chortling with glee as they said it was just right for them, in fact they'd been working out on similar ground for weeks, unbeknown to us.

Very soon some of the rather grand committee members came and swept them away from us, as of course they were the star attraction of the afternoon, the Cannon twins, and had to be introduced to the local M.F.H. and the united hunts president, and Lady Something-or-other.

Ann and I slunk into the background and went into the refreshment tent to have a sausage roll or two, and there we were found by Miss Day.

'Oh, have you lost the girls?' she said frantically, and we said, no, they'd just gone to get ready for their event.

Meanwhile the first race got under way, and there was a good deal of falling off, and riderless horses roaming about with a grin on their faces, and the usual things that happen at a point-to-point where the winner is always the one who manages to stick on longest. As we didn't know any of the people riding, or in fact any of the people milling about, we weren't terribly excited, but Miss

Day was dancing up and down and thought it was supersonic, and asked, 'When were the girls coming on?'

Well, the girls came on all right, and you should have seen them, on a pair of perfectly matched, gleaming-coated chestnuts lent for the occasion, and so spirited that they fairly danced.

'Golly!' I breathed. 'Don't they look *smashing*?'

They certainly did, and the way they handled those horses was smashing too. They were first-class and showed it.

First they gave an exhibition of pair jumping and it was out of this world, as the horses moved in step and every action of the riders was synchronized. They were just like one rider and its shadow, and as they sailed over the hedges the crowd went mad with cheering.

Then came the main race of the day, for the President's Cup, and of course all the best riders were in it because they wanted to say that they had raced with the Cannon twins. It was terrific, and as the horses came thundering up and took the last hedge, almost flying, there were Norrie and Dorrie and two fine men riders practically neck to neck.

I thought Miss Day was going to have a fit, shrieking, 'Come on, girls! Sock 'em, bash 'em, leave 'em behind!'

In the end Dorrie won by a neck, with Norrie and

a man dead-heating second. I was so excited I could feel my eyes sticking out like organ stops.

'Hurray, hurray!' shrieked Miss Day. Then to our amazement and horror she suddenly turned to Ann and me and flung her arms round our necks.

'You clever, clever girls!' she yowled. 'You marvellous girls! To think *you* taught them!'

I've had some shocks in my time, but this was the tops. That poor woman actually thought – well, Ann and I were dumb.

'Oh don't!' yelled Ann. 'Please, Miss Day! We didn't – I mean – we weren't – I mean, they – oh *gosh*!'

Meanwhile the President was coming on to the course to present the Cup, and as was the proper thing Dorrie and Norrie just shook hands with him, and stood back so that the man, who was a member of the Hunt, could have the Cup, and everybody cheered.

'Why aren't they getting the Cup?' demanded Miss Day. 'Why's that man getting it?'

We muttered something about the girls being just visitors, but she wasn't a bit pleased and rumbled on darkly about it being unfair, and we were so terrified that somebody would hear her that we dragged her off to the refreshment tent to get a cup of tea. She still kept saying, 'I don't understand –' and we felt that any minute she'd go and complain to the Committee.

However, another embarrassment arose for us. In came some people that Miss Day knew, and before we could get our breath she was introducing us to them as 'the two clever girls who taught my nieces to ride'. As these people were local riders of some repute, they looked at Ann and me with their mouths open.

'Taught the Cannon twins to ride?' somebody gasped.

'Yes, indeed,' said Miss Day, smiling like a pussy cat. 'Jill and Ann are so clever. Wonderful teachers. Dorrie and Norrie couldn't do a thing until these two took them in hand.'

By now a few more people were gathering round and staring at us, we felt awful, and wished we could crawl under a table or something. Worse was to follow. Along came a newspaper reporter and a camera man.

'Where are the girls who taught the Cannon twins to ride?'

'It's all a mistake –' began Ann in a sort of strangled voice, but it didn't do any good, because the next minute they were pulling us out into the open and arranging us, and the newspaperman was saying, 'Smile, please – get a good, full picture of them, Bill.'

There was a ring of people all round us, watching. I don't know what we looked like, but we were shaking like jellyfish, and I'm sure neither of us looked like the sort of bods to teach a three-year-old kid to ride, let alone the Cannon twins.

'Now we'll have one with our famous riders in it,' said the camera man, and along came Norrie and Dorrie giggling at us and nearly having hysterics.

'Did these girls really teach you to ride?' asked the newspaperman.

'Sure they did,' said the awful Norrie, winking at me.

'Too right, they did,' said Dorrie.

'I say, this is a scoop,' said the newspaperman. 'Cannon twins were taught to ride by two unknown British girls.'

So they got us in a row and took another photograph. Norrie and Dorrie grinned from ear to ear.

'Come on, you two,' muttered Norrie. 'Look as if you were enjoying it.'

'Can they put us in prison for this?' murmured Ann.

'If *you* didn't teach us,' said Dorrie, 'I don't know who did.'

The twins linked arms with us, the camera snapped, a lot more people came along and everybody clapped.

Miss Day was so happy she was fairly dancing about. Everybody else guessed there was something peculiar going on, knowing who the twins were, but they were all enjoying themselves so much that nobody asked any awkward questions, and the next minute – believe it or not – Ann and I were invited, along with Miss Day, to go and have tea in the Committee tent.

By now we were seeing the funny side of it too. While we nibbled gorgeous sandwiches and cakes amid the great and famous of the riding world, people kept coming up to us and winking and saying, 'Some teachers!' and things like that. And there was darling Miss Day talking to the M.F.H. and we could hear her voice above everything else saying, 'And do you know, two months ago the dear girls couldn't even mount a pony! And look at them now!'

'Marvellous!' agreed the M.F.H.

'And it's all owing to Jill and Ann,' went on Miss Day, 'so if you know of anybody else who wants to learn to ride –'

'It's all turned out wonderfully,' cried Dorrie, seizing a tray of ices and pressing them on to Ann and me. 'Aunt Maud is happy, it's the day of her life, and we've enjoyed every minute of it, and the only black spot is the thought that you'll soon be going away. It's all been such fun.'

'Yes, it has,' I agreed. 'It's been a super job for us, and everything is going to feel awfully flat after this, when we get home.'

Somebody grabbed Norrie and Dorrie and took them away, and Ann and I were left alone.

'I must say, we do get into some thrilling situations through no fault of our own, don't we?' she laughed.

'What's all this?' said a stern voice behind us.

We whizzed round, and there stood our old friend Captain Cholly-Sawcutt, the famous British rider, who had been such a help to us in the past as you know from reading my previous books.

We couldn't believe our eyes.

'Is it really you?' I gasped.

'Yes, it's really me. I'm told to come and have a look at the two wonderful girls who taught the even more wonderful Cannon twins to ride, and who do I behold but my little Chatton friends Jill and Ann! I've come across you two in some comic spots, but this beats all. How come?'

'Come over here,' said Ann, 'and we'll tell you the whole story.'

We piloted him into a corner and poured it all out. He laughed his head off.

'If your mothers knew the sort things you get yourselves into!' he chortled.

'It's just these pony jobs,' I explained. 'They always turn out unexpected. But this one's all over now, and we're going home tomorrow.'

'And we don't know what we'll do next,' said Ann sadly. 'You see, our mothers expect us to do something with a future in it. We're getting rather old now.'

Captain Cholly-Sawcutt looked serious.

'Yes, you are. Too old to play around any more. You've had lots of fun and I agree with your mothers it's high time you settled down.'

'But what are we going to *do*?' I asked. 'Because we don't know.'

'I'll tell you what you're going to do,' he said. 'You're going to get yourselves seriously trained for some proper job, and you're going to keep up your riding for a hobby. You'll always enjoy it, but you can't be kids for ever, playing around with your ponies. Now you two get back to Chatton and tell your mothers what I say, and jolly good luck with whatever profession you take up. Agreed?'

'I do think you're right,' I said. 'And whatever Mummy suggests I'll get down to it. I'll learn short-hand and typing and French and German.'

'So will I,' said Ann. 'It's a deal. This is our very last fling, and now we're going to be grown up.'

'Coo!' I said. 'I feel as if I was secretary to the Prime Minister already. Let's go and have another ice to celebrate.'